Whistler in the Dark
by John Malcolm

First published by William Collins Ltd in 1986

First paperback edition
published by Lilburne Press in 2005

Lilburne Press
22 Athelstan Road
Folkestone
Kent
CT19 6EU
01303 257 659
Email: lilburnepress@hotmail.com
www.lilburnepress.co.uk

ISBN 1 901167 12 7

The Tim Simpson Mysteries
by John Malcolm

Available from Lilburne Press in this series:

Whistler in the Dark
featuring JM Whistler
and his connections with
the Thames and the USA

£7.99
ISBN 1 901167 12 7

Circles and Squares
featuring the artists
William and Ben Nicholson
and their connections
with Bloomsbury
£7.99
ISBN 1 901167 11 9

Simpson's Homer
featuring the American artist
Winslow Homer
and his connections
with the Newcastle area
£7.99
ISBN 1 901167 14 3

The complete Tim Simpson series:-

1	A Back Room in Somers Town	8	Sheep, Goats and Soap
2	The Godwin Sideboard	9	A Deceptive Appearance
3	The Gwen John Sculpture	10	The Burning Ground
4	Whistler in the Dark	11	Hung Over
5	Gothic Pursuit	12	Into the Vortex
6	Mortal Ruin	13	Simpson's Homer
7	The Wrong Impression	14	Circles and Squares
		15	Rogues Gallery

For a detailed description of these books,
see www.fantasticfiction.co.uk, under John Malcolm.

NB His novel "Mortal Instruments" (2003) is not part of this series.

WHISTLER IN THE DARK

By

John Malcolm

CHAPTER 1

'*Nocturne in Blue and Silver,*' said Charles Massenaux happily, reclining comfortably back in his creaky swivel chair so that he could swing his leather-clad feet on to the scratched surface of his desk. 'Ah, I remember it well. A coup. A definite coup. It came in from the Eastern Front. Before we got *Harmony in White and Gold,* that was. Not to mention the etchings.'

I peered past the stained soles of his brightly-polished black shoes, up the curving pinstripe of his trouser-legs to focus on the long, pale handsome face under the smooth dark hair. There was just enough room in the little cubby-hole of his office, lined with shelved catalogues and reference books, for one visitor to squeeze into the hard spare chair between desk and wall. His feet, cocked up at high level, were too close to my face or comfort. Even his dark socks, I could see, had a vague pinstripe to them. Like many connected with the Fine Art Trade, Charles went in for the uniformed sobriety of appearance one might associate with banking or undertaking rather than the illusory panache of one involved in the disposal of expensive personal possessions.

'The Eastern Front?'

He grinned. Movements in the building behind the office wall and underneath us testified to the continuing success and bustle of Christerby's Auction Rooms in the West End. He waved a hand about him.

'This,' he said grandiloquently, 'is headquarters. The concrete bunker housing Our Führer and countless staff officers. Our Worthing premises are not, perhaps, quite so career-enhancing and, being near to Brighton, attract a lot of very dangerous flak. Very dangerous flak indeed. Fall from grace here and you are likely to tumble down to Worthing. Hence the expression: The Eastern Front. The place to which they send those officers they do not want to come back.' He smiled knowingly.

1

I clucked my tongue. 'So much for your widely-advertised Regional Policy. "The best service for all our clients—all over the country." I take it that you here at—headquarters —snatched the painting from Worthing and shot it up to London instanter?'

'Of course.' His long face affected pained surprise. 'What on earth d'you think? A Whistler is an international celebrity-market piece, Tim my boy, not a provincial daub. Full colour repro catalogue material. That and the *Harmony* and the etchings went into what we call a Special Sale along with some Impressionists. Big time stuff, some of it by his old mate Degas.' He sniffed. 'Nearly all of it went to America, of course.'

'Of course. What were they?'

'What were what?'

'The *Nocturne* and the *Harmony,* you chump. What were they? Apart from his highly affected titles?'

'Oh, I see. The *Nocturne* was a Battersea Reach job. Quite nice, actually. There was a bit of Cremorne Gardens in one corner and the old bridge. An important one. Fetched about seventy-five grand, I recall.'

'Plus Danegeld?'

His face wrinkled in distaste. 'Plus buyer's premium, yes, if that's what you mean.'

'So it really cost seventy-five thousand pounds plus ten per cent plus VAT on the ten per cent. Eighty-three thousand six hundred and twenty-five in total. You dear fellows do so conveniently like to avoid the reality of a buyer's life. And you made fifteen grand on it between buyer and seller. Not bad. What was the *Harmony?*'

He took his feet off the desk, put them under its surface and sat up to face me formally. His face stiffened; auctioneers like Christerby's get very defensive about their cut from the efficient exchange of goods via their premises. His brow furrowed as he deliberately ignored my calculations and concentrated on the last question.

2

'It was a hitherto unrecorded portrait of his early mistress, Jo Hiffernan. The red-haired Irish one who posed for the *Lady in White.*'

'Was it now? That was a coup, too, wasn't it? She was the one who posed in the famous and scandalous double-female nude by Courbet called *Le Sommeil*, I seem to recall. Unrecorded? How come?'

He warmed up a little at the flattery. He passed a modest hand over his long, smooth, thick hair to tamp down an imagined inconsistency in its flowing curve over his aristocratic head as he gave a little shrug.

'You know how it was with Whistler. Paintings scattered all over. The famous bankruptcy sale in Tite Street after the Ruskin trial and a farthing damages. Charles Augustus Howell. The Académie Carmen. The different studios, the house in The Vale; you name it. His work could have leaked out all over the place despite his notorious dislike of releasing it to patrons. Paris, London, God knows. This one was lucky for provenance—came through a relative of his brother Willie, distaff side. Been hanging unknown for years.'

'And the *Nocturne?*'

'Ah, that was an interesting one. He could hardly sell during his lifetime but there was a terrific speculative market in Whistlers after his death, pre-1914 or so. Some cove bought it off a London dealer—Agnew or perhaps Macchant—as a spec and retired to Worthing with it. Died in the 'twenties. Passed on from father to son to granddaughter. Never thought much of it; smeary blue daub, she called it. Nearly had heart failure when we sold it.'

'What widow-warmers you are. Don't tell me; you got it from a roadshow you did to cut out the local trade?'

He shook his head. 'No, she just walked in with it. Just like that. Simple as pie. But enough of us, my dear Tim; let us talk about you. This will set the trade by the ears; White's Art Investment Fund are after a Whistler. What's it to be?

3

A *Nocturne,* an *Arrangement* or a *Harmony?* I say, is something the matter?' His long face registered mock alarm.

I put a clenched fist carefully on the desk and glared at him. 'It most certainly will not set the trade by the ears! If the trade get to hear that we are after a Whistler, it will be *Discord for Knuckles and Pinstripes,* my *dear* Charles, let me tell you! This is a private conversation! I'm not alerting that bunch of vultures so that they can clamber all over the hoggin and drive prices up!'

He chuckled and held up a restraining finger. 'Now then, Tim. Enough of that. Of course I won't tell them; I was only pulling your leg. Not that you frighten me; not any more. I've heard all about you and I've watched you for the last few months. It's quite true what they say.'

'Oh? And what the bloody hell is that?'

He smiled sweetly. 'Your bark is much worse than your bite. Ever since you've been under new management. I must say that charming girl Sue Westerman has done wonders with you. What a super girl she is! I've never really understood—no, I'd better not, had I, it might cause a regression.'

'Now look here, Charles—'

'All right! All right! Take it easy! All I'm saying is that your temper seems much improved, you look better, you smile more and the trade are absolutely amazed. I met Morris Goldsworth in, the rooms last week looking quite flabbergasted; he said that you actually nodded at him. Not cordially, of course, that would be too much, but a nod nevertheless. Usually, he says, you try to hit him over the head with the nearest bureau-bookcase just because he may have outbid you for the paintings you and he clash over. And, what's more, you seem to be peacefully ensconced in the City these days, getting on with your little bit of banking and staying out of trouble. I'm very happy for you; you've settled down at last.' His teeth glinted wolfishly.

I scowled at him. 'Be very careful,' I said. 'Very careful.'

'I am. I am. All I'm observing is how temperate you've become. She's a smashing girl. Pride of the Tate Gallery. Highly professional. Done you a world of good. Must be quite hard to keep up with. We all hope you'll be very happy together.'

'Shut up!'

His smile was like the Cheshire Cat's. I got up and stood over him, squeezing round the desk. He beamed up at me.

'Thank you for your help, Charles.'

'Always a pleasure. White's Art Fund is always welcome. It's not that you're such regular buyers as some I could mention but we do enjoy the prestige.'

I gave him an affectionate prod. 'And you are the star of your Impressionist Department. I've always said that they don't really appreciate you enough here. However, enough of the mutual admiration; I have to go.'

'To pick up a Whistler? Just like that?'

'Oh no. We are an Investment Trust, Charles. We will have to agree on a fundamental decision in our investment policy. Then I will have to set about the job of implementing it. These things take time.'

'I see. You haven't actually got one in view, then?'

'Not in view, no.' The address scribbled in my notebook could hardly be called a view, so technically I was still speaking the truth. 'We'll have to shop around.'

'Ye-es.' He gave me a long, slow look. 'At least you'll be out on the open market for this one so there won't be any er, imbroglio, will there?'

I gave him, in return, a wide innocent stare. 'Of course not. And as you say, I'm settled down, aren't I? Violence is off, dear. This is just a plain, straightforward business decision. The one thing that is out of the question this time is an involvement in anything controversial or capable of inducing litigation, Charles.'

5

He raised his eyebrows at me in an expression of mock astonishment. 'How very unlike the pair of you,' he said, with a twist of the lips. 'I should have thought that a combination of Tim Simpson and Whistler would guarantee employment for the .entire legal profession.'

I gave him another prod, less affectionate this time, before closing the door. Charles is first-rate on art but you have to ignore his irreverent streak.

CHAPTER 2

Jeremy White braced himself back in his chair, stuck his hands into the pockets of his best banker's grey charcoal chalk-stripe and peered gloomily out of the long Georgian bow window at the gathering dusk of Park Lane outside. Lights were starting to glimmer across the park, beyond the moist black tree-lines silhouetted against the misty beyond. Yellow pinpricks and small bright blocks across the grassland provided a kind of distant shoreline, reminding me of Whistler's work itself. Well, I thought, much of it was inspired by London, despite all that speculation about his youth in Leningrad and its influence. Not that it was called Leningrad then; St Petersburg, it was.

'Some Yank'll snap it up,' Jeremy growled. 'Bound to, don't you think?'

'Must do,' Geoffrey Price agreed, parrot-like. 'No other Americans worth bothering about in that period, are there?'

I scowled at him. Now that he was managing director of the Park Lane set-up he occupied the elegant first-floor office that Jeremy had once used, with its long bay windows and balcony overlooking the trees. Above the mantelpiece hung one of the eighteenth-century, full-length portraits of the original White, founder of White's Bank, in his blue coat, white silk breeches, silk stockings and black buckled shoes, looking for all the world like an effeminate pomaded London dandy of the Regency instead of the sweat-stained South American timber trader that he really was. Jeremy now, as chairman of the Park Lane company, only visited for board meetings with me to accompany him as co-director responsible for the Art Investment Fund.Jeremy and I were almost proper merchant bankers now, of White's Bank in the City of London, preoccupied by many other affairs. One thing we had decided without

7

difficulty, however, was that the Art Fund lodged uncomfortably in the City; it was best installed with Geoffrey's personal financial services in Park Lane. The City is a mean place, where Scrooges and gamblers make their money; the West End is where they spend it and think about things like elegance and posterity. Art as an investment may be perfectly valid but it jostles uneasily with stock markets and exchange; we put it back in Park Lane with Geoffrey's administrative wings protectively over it and where we could still have some fun with it. What was more, as Jeremy happily pointed out, it was his duty to keep an eye on Park Lane and it meant that the three of us could lunch at the Mirabelle once a month without the slightest pang of conscience; Jeremy was deeply distressed by City restaurants.

'Whistler,' I said to Geoffrey severely, 'was only an American by accident, really.'

'Was he, poor fellow? How dreadful. Still, it happens to the best families, you know. Why, I remember a girl called Mabel something I knew once who—'

'Geoffrey.' Jeremy's voice cut him off as he gave an abrupt swing of his blond patrician head. 'I think Tim has something to tell us.'

'Sorry. Fire away, Tim.'

I gave him a reproachful half-grin. Jeremy was in a somewhat testy mood that evening. There was nothing wrong with Geoffrey Price's management of the Park Lane office, where we had all started out together; it was sound and competent if rather too prudent for Jeremy's taste. The administration of White's Art Investment Fund, a scheme Jeremy and I had founded for investors wanting to put longer-term money into art and antiques without actually having to buy a Rembrandt themselves, was impeccable. Jeremy and I bought the Fund's investments and Geoffrey managed the paperwork; it suited all of us. The Art Fund was only a small part of Geoffrey's responsibilities, though; since Jeremy and I had moved to the City, he looked after the business

8

Jeremy had originally founded to take care of people's personal investments. Like many born to inherited wealth, Jeremy had a strong attachment to the preservation of it. His expertise in side-stepping the methods various British governments have devised to wrest wealth from individuals, whether inherited or earnt, had provided the basis of a very successful business involving bond-broking, insurance, tax havens, capital transfer schemes and many other enjoyable ways of thwarting the Inland Revenue. His family, the staunch, conservative, parsimonious and immobile Whites of White's Bank, had disapproved strongly of Jeremy's success; they regarded him as an upstart, a pushy young cousin from a cadet branch who ought to have known his place, low down in the pecking order. Unfortunately for them the Bank had managed its affairs badly and Jeremy, co-opted by his friends in the big insurance companies who owned some of the Bank's shares, had entered the citadel at last and was on the board of directors despite their resistance.

It was proving to be a testing time for him. In some ways Jeremy had taken to the Bank like a duck to water. The City is all about land and gambling; for someone of Jeremy's background, land and gambling were so much part of the bloodstream that hardly' any thought, only reflex action, was required. Unfortunately, the early nineteen-eighties were not perhaps the best years for small, traditional, inherited merchant banks. Many of them have disappeared or have been swallowed up by the big clearing banks and others. I could think of Brandts, who came a cropper over Harrods of Buenos Aires years ago, or Anthony Gibbs, who were painfully digested by the Honkers and Shankers after some nasty losses. The thought came to me that both Brandts and Gibbs had originally had South American connections like White's and that, in the end, it had not done them much good.

9

'It was his grandfather,' I said. 'Impecunious Anglo-Irish stock, Ulster cadet branch of decent English family. Committed the unpardonable social error of enlisting as a private soldier in a regiment in which his grander cousin was an officer. Sir Grisly Whistler, or whatever his name was—no, Sir Kensington Whistler, that was it—came from Goring or Reading, didn't approve at all. To get rid of the problem he had his kinsman sharply transferred to another regiment which was shipping for the colonies, where there was a war on.'

'America?'

'Arrived in time to surrender at Saratoga with General Johnny Burgoyne. Not a very edifying experience.'

'Lost his trunk, doubtless,' said Geoffrey humorously, smiling until he caught out withering glances. Accountants really should not try humour; it doesn't suit them at all.

'It can't have been very cheering. He got back to England after the Declaration of Independence and then committed a further social error. He married an English girl called Anne Bishop whose father, Sir Edward, was not amused to have her joined to an impecunious ex-soldier back in disgrace from the Americas, even if he had become a colour sergeant by the time he finished. I'll say one thing for Grandpa Whistler, though; he didn't sit about whingeing, he got the message and he sailed straight back to America with his bride. He joined the American Army, had about fifteen children and served against the British in the war of 1812. Quite a lad, really.'

Geoffrey frowned in disapproval. 'Served against us? Typical. Blasted colonials. Totally unreliable once they leave here. Look at Australia. Why—'

'No, let us *not* look at Australia.' Jeremy was still testy. 'Not on any account do I ever again want to look at Australia: I find Tim's habit of storing odd biographical details of this sort in his devious mind quite endearing

10

but I do hope that soon, perhaps, in the fullness of time, he may lead us to the point he is going to make about why we should buy this Whistler.'

I put on a suitably chastened look. 'Sorry, Jeremy. I'll cut it short. One of the fifteen children was Major George Washington Whistler—three of them joined the army and three married into it, which rather followed the English family's tradition of becoming parsons or soldiers—and he became such a distinguished railroad engineer that the Tsar of Russia invited him to build the St Petersburg to Moscow railway. He was James Whistler's father and that's why James, or Jimmy as they called him, was educated in Russia for a while. His mother was Major Whistler's second wife; the first one died after having two children.'

'By "his mother" you mean the one in the famous painting?'

'I do indeed. She was a McNeill, descended from Scots Highland stock and her father took the English side in the War of Independence. The point I am trying to make is that Whistler, although born in America, was of very British genetic strains. Indeed, his irreligious Anglo-Celtic character, which was irreverent, sharp-witted, lazy, busy, self- indulgent, charming and prickly by turns, is very typical of certain British types. I use the word British in its widest sense, of course. After he left America at the age of twenty- three he never went, back; despite his bitter criticism of everything English, he could only live in France for brief periods because the best setting for him was undoubtedly London. But that's not the real point, either. The fact is that it wasn't only Oscar Wilde, another Anglo-Irishman, who learnt so much from Jimmy Whistler. He and his pupil, Sickert, also a semi-foreigner, are the two key figures in bringing over the revolution of French art that changed our own Victorian painting. Indeed, there is an argument that the Fund, if it is to have truly important,

11

representational historical British art works, should own paintings by both Whistler *and* Sickert.'

'Bravo.' Jeremy stood up crisply. 'Admirably put. I'm convinced. Not only that; since we own the terra-cotta figure of Gwen John modelled by Rodin for the Whistler's Muse memorial sculpture, I do feel very strongly that it is very appropriate that we own a Whistler. After all, Gwen John was a pupil of Whistler's as well. Wasn't she?'

'Yes, Jeremy.'

'Approved then, Geoffrey? You'll record, will you, that Tim has approval to proceed with negotiations for the purchase? Around one hundred thousand pounds with discretion. Final sum to be approved by the Trustees, as usual. Right?'

'Right.'

'All I say, as I did when we began, is that there is a fair chance that a Yank will snap it up for a ridiculous sum. You know how it is; they seem to have unlimited funds for this sort of thing.'

'Certainly if the Freer Gallery got wind of it, or anyone like them,' I said, 'we'd be left at the post. I'll get on to it right away.'

'Good.' Jeremy looked at his watch. 'Tim, we really have to talk about other matters very urgently tomorrow. In my office, first thing? At the Bank?'

'OK, Jeremy.'

'Good. I'm off. Until tomorrow, then.' That spoiled it. Geoffrey gave me a significant look. He'd doubtless heard rumours on the grapevine. What he didn't know was how much work it meant for me and that it was going to affect him rather radically. The work was not so much on paper but in the brain and it would have to be followed by some careful handling of Jeremy. It made me very preoccupied as I left the Park Lane office. As I came out I saw, with pleasure, a No. 30 bus heave into sight. It felt just like old times, to go upstairs and bowl down Knightsbridge, past Harrods and the

12

Victoria and Albert Museum before turning into the Old Brompton Road so that I could drop off at the corner of Onslow Gardens.

CHAPTER 3

Her involvement started, as so many things do, with a domestic wrangle.

'I do not eat bran for breakfast,' I said firmly. 'Just as I do not eat nasty coarse brown bread with wood chips and pieces of hardboard in it. That sort of brown toast ruins the taste of the marmalade. Stifles it altogether. You have to have white toast to taste marmalade and marmalade — proper orange marmalade — is what breakfast is all about.'

'My, but we are grumpy this morning.'

'Merely to defend an honest breakfast of the sort everyone has been eating for ages does not justify an accusation of grumpiness. The way everyone witters on about high fibre nowadays has a positively sanctimonious ring about it.'

She compressed her lips as she glanced at the bran and the muesli.

'Porridge, now, that's another matter, If ever there was a decent way of consuming one's oats, porridge must be it. With syrup and cream, of course.'

A furrow began to crease the space between her brown eyebrows. Her blue eyes took on an unblinking, accusatory stare.

'All I did was offer you some bran. There's no need to go off the deep end.'

'No, you did not just "offer" me some bran. Don't try to pretend you are all sweet reasonableness and that I am the bone-headed trampler of the Rational Little Woman. What you did was to say that you thought that I "ought" to eat some nasty disgusting bran and you plonked down that block of unmilled loose-packed chipboard you call a granary loaf with a derogatory remark about my favourite pre-sliced white toaster.'

'I knew that you were going to be unpleasant. I could tell from last night. You came in with a face like an old

14

boot, spent the evening muttering and went irritably to sleep as soon as you got into bed.'

'So you decided to try and slip me some nasty medicine this morning.'

'I was concerned for your health. I have been reading—'

'That utter rubbish that so-called health articles spout about diet. You'll say next that a man of my, er, stocky build and constitution is a prime suspect for heart attacks, cerebral haemorrhage, incontinence, palsy, prostate problems and God knows what else unless he eats that godforsaken bowel fodder.'

'Aha! Aha! So you have been reading some of it! Well you said it, Tim, not me.'

'I did indeed. And utter rubbish it is, too. These medical fashions are ridiculous. I remember that when I was at College there was a big scare about the Boat Club because ex-oarsmen were supposed to get fatty degeneration of the heart tissues when they stopped their boating. Everyone got quite worked up about it until some oarsman or other found an old treatise called "The Longevity of Boat Race Oarsmen" written by an ancient old Blue in the medical profession who'd traced everyone who ever rowed for Oxford or Cambridge since Victoria came to the throne or some similar date. It turned out from his statistics that they live for twenty years longer than anyone else so that was the end of that. Mind you, he could have saved himself all the statistical work, I reckon. Should have thought it was obvious to anyone who's ever been to Henley Regatta.'

She shook her head at me sadly. 'So you think the same applies to Old Rugger Blues too? Oarsmen always seem much stringier types to me.'

'Possibly. Not the same men of sound bottom that we are.'

There was a pause. I looked at the breakfast table, brightened by the sun streaming in from Onslow Gardens outside, the packets she'd carefully put out, the teapot, the table clutter and felt a sharp pang of remorse. Her good intentions were getting a severe mauling and I was behaving in the worst possible domestic tradition. She sat across the table and cocked her head as she gave me a reproachful glance. Her brown hair was brushed to one side of her face and the normally large eyes glinted in a slight compression. The generous mouth was neutral, carefully avoiding any giveaway quirk of the lips. A stiff blouse, tucked into a neat skirt, gave her the crisp, competent look that has always been her hallmark; Sue is one of those very English girls, cool-surfaced, outwardly slender and carefully buttoned- down, that make you think of brisk teachers, head prefects and we-know-best. It can be very irritating.

Don't get me wrong; Sue is the greatest thing that ever happened to me and she is certainly not cool under the surface, quite molten in fact, but outward appearances count for a lot with Sue's sort. Sue's sort; that would infuriate her. I know that she's unique but I'm just trying to give you a picture of her; there is a type, a sort, a genre, if that's the right word, into which Sue potentially falls. It's a teacher-type. I mean she certainly isn't a punk or a raver or a Monroe, she's a controlled, well-educated, intelligent, well-behaved, sophisticated girl from a good family who isn't a Sloane Ranger or a Green Ranger or whatever they call County girls now, or any other modish type. Which is why I care for her more than somewhat, I suppose.

I looked round'at the fresh-papered walls of the sunny room and thought with amusement of the paintings of her own that she'd steadily inserted between mine as our time together had passed. This was the second go we'd had at living together; it followed a year she'd spent away in Australia during which various events, best forgotten, had occurred. The flat in Onslow Gardens was still new for us; we'd had only a few months of occupancy. Where I had carefully hung my still life by

16

Alan Gwynne-Jones and a sketch of a soldier by Orpen, she'd put a Hockney print in between, one she'd had for a long time. Over my black-and-white etching of Dorelia by Augustus John she'd hung a print by Picasso of a geometrically dismembered nude woman. Next to my ink sketch of RAF pilots in a wartime briefing room by Seago she'd hung a fabulous watercolour of a suburban angel sitting in a garden full of washing hung out to dry, by Stanley Spencer. War and Peace, she called the duo, with a significant roll of the eyes to indicate whose was whose and the relative roles they implied. She hadn't managed to oust my big Victorian coastal marine by Clarkson Stanfield from its key position over the mantelpiece — she disapproves strongly of romantic Victorian painting — but she'd managed to tuck in her still life of glasses on a table by Sylvia Gosse and her Laura Knight — a circus — and a fine Dod Proctor and an Elizabeth Stanhope Forbes to such good effect that the ladies were strongly represented on every wall. Above the sideboard at the far end of the room I had hung a smashing watercolour by Wilson Steer, one of his radiant views of the shore at Bosham, a great water-landscape that sang with colour and space. Next to it, very carefully, Sue had hung an interior by Ethel Walker, an exact antithesis of my open-air Steer. It was an oil depicting a girl in a white dress standing in a fireplace, a pure derivation from Whistler but looser in handling. Looking at the two paintings, which somehow and contrarily went together surprisingly well, some idea of the force that Whistler was, the effect that his personality and work had had on our art came to me. The Ethel Walker was straight from *The Little White Girl;* even the Steer, with its barges stuck in the foreground sand, the wide watery sweep of estuary beyond, the tiny clump of church- huddled buildings in the distance and its slightly Oriental feel, was Whistler too.

I looked back at Sue. She'd been right about my preoccupation the night before. Was I getting a bit tedious for her? Without excitement, without outside stimulation perhaps, was she starting to concentrate on me, not my personality but the trivia of behaviour, diet, everyday irritating habit?

Her expression had a glaze of preoccupation on it, of distraction. That's when I thought of it.

'Sue,' I said, in mollifying tones, 'what are you doing this afternoon?'

She gave me a suspicious stare. No reply issued from her 'I thought,' I went on, uncomfortably, 'that we might have a very restrained sandwich for lunch together and that you might then like to come down the road with me to look at something.'

'Down the road? To look at something?'

'It, um, it may not actually be there, but it's supposed be a Whistler. Quite your sort of thing, really.'

The teaspoon she had picked up absently from her saucer froze in mid-air.

'A what? Whistler? What Whistler? Which one?'

'Don't be so aggressive! I had a rather strange phone-call a day or so ago from an odd old josser who said that he'd got my name from a newspaper that had an article on art investment in it. He said that he was very interested to learn that we specialized in British art and antiques, particularly nineteenth-century art. He said that he had information about a Whistler painting in private hands, an important one, and would we be interested because it's for sale. I've arranged to meet him; it's not far from you, dreaming your life away in the Tate. Turn right on Millbank and keep going along the river till you get to Chelsea Reach, then inwards for a pace or two. Would you like to come?'

I'd scored a bullseye; I could tell from the look on her face. She was as hooked as a fish with a tine through its lip. She stared at me, still suspicious.

'What do you want me for?'

'Well, now. There you are, an expert on your modern British painting, Tate Gallery, got a couple of his in

18

there haven't you, should have thought you'd be interested.'   ..:

The spoon was still frozen. 'Interested. I see. You wouldn't be wanting me to, say, authenticate it, would you?'

'Ah well, if you think you'd like to give an expert opinion, then of course I'm sure we'd be glad to, er —'

'Pay me a fee?' 'Yes. Of course.'

'There wouldn't be any trouble with that? The Fund would approve?'

'Oh yes, expert opinion, we always pay for that.'

'I know, but in view of our, that is, me and you —'

'Oh no. No problem. I have discretion, within reasonable limits, to pay such fees and it's not as though we're actually, you know, er —'

'Related in any way? Not married, for example?'

'Er, no.' Trouble, I thought, here comes trouble.

'So it's all right for you to pay your mistress for professional services but eyebrows might be raised if, say, you kept employing your wife for such things?'

Jesus, women can be contentious; always testing the edges of territory, pushing the boundary fences that little bit further into your ground, just to see how far they can go. Especially teacher-types with a vaguely feminist bent. The implications contained in her words were quite nasty; corruption; paid lechery, nepotism and, God knows, marital blackmail. The reason why Sue and I were not married went way back to decisions entirely of her own, desires to be independent she had, uncertainties about me, divorced once already, but from her words you would have thought that I was holding out in some way. The tableau painted by her remarks was so very opposite to reality that I had to put my foot down.

'Now look here, Sue! Stop giving me bloody trouble, will you? I just thought it would be nice if we had the chance to do something together this afternoon, something pleasant that would interest you. I know I've

19

had a lot of work at the Bank and have been somewhat distrait. I thought we could work together for once.'

She started to tap the side of her cup with the spoon, looking at me steadily. It sets my nerves right on edge, that does, and I glared at her.

'Don't do that! It's very irritating. You did it once before in the Tate buffet when you were making up your mind about me in some way and looking at me like something dredged up from the Thames at low tide.'

She put the spoon down quickly and, leaning across, too my hand. 'I'm sorry, Tim. Really I am. It's just that the last time I went out with you to look at paintings remember what happened? Not very nice was it? In Motcomb Street?'

'Oh, come on, Sue, that was two years or so ago. Poor old Willie Morton. It was pure chance. Couldn't happen again. I mean, could it?'

She looked at me knowingly. 'Tim Simpson, you attract trouble like a jampot does wasps. Look what you've got into since then. You seek trouble, you do.'

'I do not! Really I don't! Anyway, everyone is saying how changed I am, how quiet life is. I'm so amiable these days; Sunny Tim, they call me.'

'Who does?'

'Everyone. Why only yesterday Charles Massenaux was saying that now that you and I —'

I stopped. That look had come into her eyes again.

'Charles? Charles said what? You and I what?'

'Oh, nothing, you know, just a — well, just a —'

'Just a nice reference to Tim and Sue, eh, the paired-off couple, the settled life?"

'No, no. He was saying what a lot of good you've done me. Nothing of that anti-feminist stuff about being half of a pair that would upset you. Rather the opposite, in fact. Individuality fully preserved and all that, that —

'Tim!'

'Sorry. Look. I've got an important meeting this morning. I'm not looking forward to it, you see.'

20

'More important than us?'

I looked her straight in the face. 'Us? "Me" you mean, don't you? More important than me? "Us" is not a go-er with you; hence your objection to Charles's remarks. Staying loose, you are, as the Americans would say. Not time to commit yourself yet. I mean, you're here with me which is very nice and all that but it's a free-wheeling arrangement, isn't it?'

Her eyes were on the plate in front of her. 'You are in a foul mood this morning. You promised me we wouldn't discuss that subject for a while. You promised.'

'Sorry. Very sorry. But I don't deliberately get violent and you are important to me. Please will you come to Chelsea with me?'

She smiled softly. 'Of course I will. I'm sorry too; it was all very silly of me. I'll come.'

'Splendid. I must be off. I'll meet you at the Tate at one. Then it'll be wagons west to Battersea Reach. OK?'

She nodded. 'OK. How exciting! I've been waiting for you to ask me to come and look at paintings with you for weeks, you know.'

My father, in one of his rare confidential outbursts to me, once said, 'Tim, my boy, you'll never be able to think like a woman, understand that, it's bloody impossible.'

How right he was; I shook my head all the way to South Kensington Tube station.

CHAPTER 4

The City has never been one of my favourite haunts. I don't suppose many Americans are particularly fond of Wall Street. By the City I mean, of course, that part of the City of London which contains the banks, the brokers, the insurance men and the money-changers generally. There's a sort of Puritan streak in my nature, as there was in Whistler's, induced in my case by an upbringing and parentage that instructed me to revere work, real work, as an activity in which you make things, or grow them or deliver them or sell them. I never thought I'd wind up working for a bank; my attitude was somehow wrong.

Take White's for instance; I could admire the original White enormously. He sailed up the Amazon, found timber, got it out, sailed it back, unloaded it, sawed it up, sold it, everything. There wasn't any part of the business that he wouldn't have known and he certainly wasn't much of a banker. Like many of London's older establishments, the original description of White's had been 'merchants and bankers'; it only got shortened to Merchant Bankers later. The Whites of Jeremy's generation and those of his father and uncle before him still kept the timber trade going as part of the Bank's activities, but they never actually looked at much timber physically. The overseas companies did, but not the Bank, there in London. When Jeremy's uncle used to say that they were in the timber trade, what he meant was that they handled the documents connected with it. They didn't actually cut down trees, load them on ships, unload them or saw them up. The nearest they got to a tree by way of trade was a piece of paper. And for handling that paper and providing the finance for part of the time they made more money than those who sweated and heaved and drove and navigated and sawed. It seemed all wrong to me.

As I walked up Gracechurch Street from Monument

that morning I had a quiet ruminate on what I thought I really was doing. The key to it all lay with Jeremy. If it hadn't been for Jeremy I would still have been treadling away conscientiously for the business consultants I was with until I met him. Jeremy had got his accounts and systems into a mess, so, typical Jeremy, he simply called us in to sort them out, much as he would have got a mechanic to his car or plumber to his drains. The detail of business systems was intensely boring to Jeremy; making money and preserving it were his passions. After I had helped to sort things out and recruit Geoffrey Price, Jeremy was reluctant to see me go. He and I had a common interest in art investment and in antiques of all sorts. He thought we should do something about it. Hence the Art Investment Fund. Let's have some fun, Jeremy had said; leave your serious-minded consultants, join us, run the Fund, act as a general business member of the Park Lane company. Life was boring just then and my divorce from Carol, my ex, still fresh in mind. It was time for a change, the right moment exactly. I joined Jeremy.

One thing had led to another and now Jeremy was on the main Board of the Bank, here in the City, and I was an Associate Director, which sounds fine but doesn't really mean much, just a sort of well-paid shotgun guard, visiting fireman and general factotum to Jeremy, who was on his way up through the somewhat moribund bunch of family remnants still clinging to their directorships. Apart from one or two cousins and a relative by marriage called Peter Lewis, there were no dynastic rivals to Jeremy but he had only just got started at the Bank, so it was early days yet. Big vultures were wheeling about over the City, snapping up old merchant banks like White's; it was going to be a close run thing for survival. We had good reason to be preoccupied.

I walked in through the large Cuban mahogany doors that flank the entrance to the Bank and winked at the flunkied doorman as I passed. He grinned back and gave me a mock-salute, much less reverent than the black-suited major-domo inside, who bid me good morning with gravity. The major-domo was covering his bets; he was never quite sure about me and how seriously to take me, not being one of the family, but knowing me as Jeremy's henchman and potential dagger man, he had to play safe. I dumped my briefcase in my little office upstairs, picked up some relevant papers and strolled down the passage to find the Golden Boy himself. His office was not far from mine but it was much larger, as befitted a member of the family who, despite all entrenched opposition, had taken his seat on the main Board of Directors.

Jeremy White was, now, in his early forties; a tall, blond, patrician figure. In the States his age might have been held against him and even the City is used to seeing its whizz-kids come on much younger, but not White's; in White's the tradition of working one's way up, painful department by painstaking department, overseas posting by overseas posting, had died hard, as it many old banks. The British tradition of dead men's shoes, Buggins's turn, had persisted for too long. Jeremy had circumvented all that with the Park Lane success; he, two cousins, and Peter Lewis in Singapore were regard as the Young Turks who were doing a cut-and-slash - operation in efforts to preserve the Bank. Only in White's, thought, would a man in his mid-forties be regarded as Young Turk; it was rather like politics.

Actually, a lot of people have no idea what a merchant banker really does. They simply think of him as something grey in the City. If he is young, he is bound to be something of a cad; the seducer in a Mills and Boon romance, the one who tries to get the heroine's knickers off while she estranged from the decent young farmer who loves her. If he is old, he is bound to be disgustingly rich and something of a twister. Otherwise they have no concept of him. How he actually spends his time is a mystery. Well, merchant bankers are people who manoeuvre blocks of money in order to make a margin for themselves. They either lend money to companies they trust at a given interest rate or they help companies to raise money by getting a lot of other to put it up. For this they charge a fee. They also gamble on shares and securities, they run bank accounts and they gamble on foreign currencies, foreign shares and securities or property. They get involved in foreign trade from financial point of view. They put people in contact with one another and they help people to buy someone else's company. Alternatively they help companies to stop other people from buying them. They invest money in commodities like rubber or cocoa or gold or peanuts. You could say that they do almost anything to make a buck without actually having to manufacture anything. They are not very popular.

'Tim!' Jeremy waved me in vigorously. 'Have some coffee. We're going to need it. I've asked Clara to make it very strong this morning.'

'Thanks.' I helped myself and sat down opposite him, waiting for my preoccupations of the night before to start emerging. He smoothed down his foulard silk tie, brushed imaginary crumbs off his banker's grey charcoal worsted and peered at me apprehensively over the top of his bone china coffee cup. It was a familiar look. Jeremy and I knew each other, now, very well and I would have betted that he knew how our conversation would run within very close degrees of accuracy. Yet it said something about the man that he never assumed, never presumed, that what he thought or anticipated would necessarily come from those in whom he confided. Each occasion was separate, distinct of itself. Surprises might occur and the independence of opinion which he valued above all else must be allowed to be given full play. He might occasionally blurt his own views in an aggressive or forthright manner, but he would never expect that to dismay the expression of opposing views. Jeremy may be an autocrat but he is not an authoritarian; the expression of conventional, cautious opinion siding with some sort of conformity is anathema to his original, almost eccentric and clever mind.

'We've been here for almost six months,' he said abruptly, swerving the bone china coffee cup back to its saucer on his green leather desk-top with a flourish.

'Correct.'

'The place is a disaster. The four main activities— banking, corporate finance, investment and overseas operations—are all jumbled up with no clear lines of authority.'

'Right.'

He put his head back, nodded hopefully at my assent, and went on. 'Old James is going great guns in Brazil and Peter Lewis is fast expanding in Singapore. Pretty soon this London office will be irrelevant if we don't watch out. While we're bickering over succession they'll declare UDI and sail off quite independently of us, just like any damned colony.'

'Agreed.'

'We know how the London merchant banking scene changing. Ten years behind New York. The Americans the Japanese are vast. They make us look puny. I cottoned on to the fact that this is a big international in which trading and salesmanship are all-important ago. They're setting up vast international investment supermarkets that cover everything. There are people who think that banks like ours can survive by becoming—what they call it—specialist boutiques? A sort of Ye Olde Sweete Shoppe approach. Well, to blazes with that.

'Hear, hear. That's defeatist talk.'

He stiffened up visibly in encouragement. I could see that he was really working himself up a bit but I was in total agreement with him so far. The only thing that worried me was whether he had thought the whole thing through 'At least, Jeremy,' I said, 'we can try to become a decent regional supermarket with some specialist lines, not just sort of fly-blown corner grocer's shop. To carry the analogy as far as I want to.'

He smacked his hand onto his desk-top, rattling the cups. 'That's right! A decent regional network with its own strengths!'

I took a careful pull at my coffee. It was very good, being Brazilian and culled from the Bank's own properties, down Curitiba way. 'All unwittingly,' I said mildly, 'or perhaps wittingly and instinctively, that's what the Park Lane operation has taken some steps towards. It was the right direction. It's not exactly a Merrill Lynch or a Nomura but it's a start. Offices in twelve carefully selected cities outside London. Range of investment services and advice for clients. Christ knows how long your uncle resisted it before we prised him out. Mind you, a lot of other traditional London merchant bankers don't like the idea either. Nevertheless, look at Hambro Life.'

'Oh, *Hamburgs!* Don't let's talk about them! It's Park Lane I wanted to discuss.' His face suddenly twisted in an expression of tensioned distress. 'Come on, Tim. I need your advice now. No bullshit.'

He had thought it through. And he hadn't liked the logical conclusion. Jeremy is essentially kind-hearted; he likes to do the right thing by his loyal supporters. Loyalty is something that Jeremy will never forget, even in his quite ruthless drive to dominate and preserve his family's bank. He likes those around him to be happy, smiling, so he can look around and say, 'Look at them, my gang, great.' Members of his gang were entitled to Jeremy's absolute protection from grief of any kind. I hesitated; I like Geoffrey Price, always have. I met Sue through him.

'Geoffrey is an accountant with a capital A. I think he even loves double-entry bookkeeping as a sort of pure science mixed with philosophy. But we will have to expand the Park Lane network. Geoffrey is a great MD at the current level but he's no salesman, certainly not for a big selling operation of the sort I'm sure we're both thinking of. We need a fast, nasty insurance-type sales director who wants at least a hundred grand a year and a growing empire to satisfy his ego drive. That's not Geoffrey. There are other places for Geoffrey but I know what you're thinking; he'll be very disappointed.'

He let out a long sigh, mainly of relief; partly of sadness, then he brightened. 'Thank God it's not just me. Tim, I'm frightfully glad you think that way too. Of course Geoffrey'll be much better employed here at the Bank and eventually much happier too. Good. Look, we'll draw up an action plan later because we haven't time this morning due to this strange American that James has sent us, but we'll finalize it in two days' time. Is that all right?'

What he meant was would I draw up the action plan in my spare time between now and then so that he could edit and approve it. I nodded as cheerfully as emotion would allow and he rushed round to pour me another cup of coffee himself; like a man who as just shed a severe burden.

'Splendid. I must say that having old Larkfield as a temporary chairman might have been a lot worse. At least he's an experienced stockbroker and he understands what I mean when I say we'll have to go into wholesaling as a minimum if we're to survive. Probably a link with a stock-jobber, like Warburg's have with Akroyd and Smithers.'

The appointment of Lord Larkfield as a temporary chairman after the forced departure of Jeremy's uncle, Sir Richard White, had at first been a cause for gloom. In fact the breathing space had been very useful while the contenders for internal power at the Bank gathered their forces. Until recently, merchant banks had been forbidden to have links with Stock Exchange firms but the game is fast changing; we were going to have to change, too.

Jeremy babbled happily on, now that all was clear in his mind. 'It's going to be a time of great stimulation, Tim. It really is. There'll be tremendous opportunities for everyone; Geoffrey will soon see that. It'll be much better for him, professionally I mean, to be near the financial end of things. You're absolutely right about the sales aspect. I tell you what; there's an absolutely red-hot man at—'

One thing about Jeremy; he's an unfailing optimist. It might well be that events could scupper the Bank for ever or that a bold venture into wider distribution and selling might overreach itself but such qualms were for the fainthearted only. Jeremy has always seen his world in expansive terms. I wondered by what quirk of genetics the Whites had managed to turn up another merchant adventurer in a cadet branch and decided that pure statistics probably had something to do with it.

'At least,' he said, 'I'm feeling in a better mood to meet this man. James seems to think it'll be worth our while, but he's so damn cryptic these days; I've no idea what we're supposed to do. Just know that he is one of our transatlantic cousins and we should see him.' He sat back, coffee in hand, with a rapt look on his face. 'Who knows what life is

CHAPTER 5

Jeremy's secretary, Clara, came surging in with a visiting card more or less on schedule. The marriage of Jeremy to his uncle's secretary, Mary, had been very useful to him for a few brief months after Sir Richard left; Mary knew the Bank's workings inside out and she'd steered us past some dangerous rocks. But now she was happily pregnant, managing Jeremy during the day by remote control from their London house. His new secretary, Clara, had bounced up by promotion from a floor below. She was a big jolly girl with a County background but perfectly discreet manners when not in the vicinity of a horse.

'Mr Casey is here' she said, handing Jeremy the card. 'Shall I show him in?'

He glanced at it, closed his eyes, and handed it to me without a word. 'Andrew O'Brien Casey,' it said. 'Vice President, Owens, McLeod and Casey. Investment Bankers.' An address in Chicago's Loop district followed, which half-surprised me; an old-fashioned firm, I thought.

'Sure now,' I said, handing the card back, 'would that be the Cork Caseys or the County Wicklow bunch, d'you think?'

He grimaced. 'The Chicago Caseys. Can you imagine? A Welshman, a Scotsman and an Irishman setting up a bank in Chicago? It's like a bar-room joke.'

I grinned at him and he smiled back, still showing relief at the decision over Geoffrey. I'd read the file on his desk. It was indeed a Welshman, a Scotsman and an Irishman who set up the original firm of Owens, McLeod and Casey in the mid-nineteenth century to deal in cattle, hides and leather goods in the Chicago area. Then they found somehow that they had to get involved in the shipment of their own goods across the Great Lakes. That got them financing other cargoes; wheat, farm produce, bulk materials. From there it was a short

30

step to becoming an investment bank, financing the Mid-West's burgeoning industries. In some ways there were parallels with White's own development, except that their continent had been busy enough to keep them fully occupied. They were not big by American standards, nothing like the giants of New York, but they were big enough by ours. I'd never heard of them outside the USA before.

Jeremy turned to Clara. 'Very well. Show him in, will you?' He pushed our cups across the desk at her. 'And a fresh lot of these, please. Americans are somewhat fussy about coffee; you'd better weaken the brew down a bit, my dear girl.'

She gave me a faint wink as she tidied up and then, the decks suitably cleared for action, ushered in our first mid-west banker of the day, or come to that, of the month.

He was young. Well, he was about my age; mid-thirties. It was a surprise. Anyone who'd got on well with such a crusty old buzzard as James White in Brazil would naturally have been pigeonholed in a locker of advanced age to my thinking. But he wasn't. He was tall, lean, brown-haired; at least two inches taller than me—say about six foot three—and wore a dark suit of inexpensive type, a white shirt and an undistinguishable—to me—club tie. I recognized his black brogues; they were a good quality Florsheim wingtip number of about two years ago that cost fifty dollars then. There was nothing flash or expensive about Mr Casey; he carried an executive briefcase with a combination lock, had clear blue eyes that looked straight at you and was obviously in very fit condition. His freckled skin glowed with health.

'How d'you do?' inquired Jeremy, at his most genial self. 'May I introduce Tim Simpson, my Associate Director?'

'Gentlemen.' The American's grasp was firm, as I'd expected, without overdoing it. 'It's very kind of you to see me.' His voice was strong and well-pitched but he gave me a quick glance, almost of surprise.

'Not at all.' Jeremy was still at his courteous peak. 'The pleasure is ours. Coffee? Splendid. My cousin James—well, he's a very remote cousin really, the Brazilian branch of the family, you know—told us to look out for you when you got to London, so of course you're most welcome.'

I smiled inwardly at that. Curmudgeonly old James White had no opinion of the London office and even less of the country as a whole, which in his view was suffering from too much democracy and the effects of the Welfare State. He was having a tremendously forceful last few years in office, enjoying himself hugely with deals and finances in Brazil which would have given most financiers a heart attack. It was almost as if he was deliberately showing off to us. Look, he seemed to be saying, you idle, lazy, boring lot, look what I'm doing in very difficult circumstances and tell me if you can teach me anything.

Casey smiled as he sipped his coffee. 'I certainly enjoyed meeting with James White. A remarkable man.'

'Indeed. Have you just arrived in London?'

Casey put down his cup carefully before replying. 'Two days ago. I had some things to discuss with a number of US commercial bank branches here.'

'Oh, so at least you've had time to recover from that long, tiring flight.' Jeremy was all solicitude; you'd think he'd done the journey himself.

'Oh yes.' Casey folded his hands, big hands they were, over each other and separated them again. 'I suppose that James White indicated that I wanted a brief discussion with you on this package, this remarkable package, that you've put together for the State Railroad?'

'Well,' said Jeremy cautiously, 'he did sort of indicate that, yes, although he didn't advise what specifically. It's why Tim's here. It's a particular baby of his.'

The American looked at me with a faint smile on his lips. 'Forgive me for saying that I'm a bit surprised, although I think that James must have mentioned your name. I had more associated you with art and antiques than railroad deals.'

Jeremy clapped his hands. 'Bravo! You see, Tim, your notoriety is spreading. Quite right! But I should explain that the Art Fund, in which Tim and I are closely involved, is a very small part of our investment programme. Tim has, as it happens, a particular personal interest in South American railways because his father was involved in them.'

'Oh really?' Casey's voice carried real interest. 'In Brazil?'

'Only in a small way. He was mainly with BAGS—sorry, the Buenos Aires and Great Southern. Then he was in Peru.'

Casey waved one of his big hands. 'So you know all about that area, then?'

'As it happens, Parrivale Electronics was a client of mine when I was a consultant. Before joining the Bank. They make signalling systems, very sophisticated ones. When the São Paulo and Minas Gerais State Railways put out for tender for signalling systems, James White had been playing golf with the director. The Falklands helped, as he probably told you.'

A look of incomprehension crossed Casey's face. 'The Falklands? Helped? No, he didn't. How was that?'

'Oh yes. It's one of those apocryphal stories that go the rounds. Don't ask me if it's really true. An RAF Vulcan bomber force-landed at Rio during the war, short of fuel. That's all on record. In Brazil, as with most South American countries, the Army and the Air Force report direct to the President because they can be a source of revolution, or a coup d'etat. The Navy is a separate entity with its own Secretary; sailors out at sea are not usually a threat to the Presidential palace. Well, the Army-Air Force didn't pick up the intruding Vulcan on their radar detection equipment, which, as it happens, wasn't British. The Brazilian Navy, whether because of long associations with the Royal Navy or perhaps in memory of Lord Cochrane, had a British system. One of their destroyers off Rio harbour did pick up the Vulcan and kept flashing the land-based lot that they should be on the alert. By the time the Navy had screamed blue murder at the Air Force and they scrambled their fighters, the Vulcan was landing at Galeão. So one of the railway directors said jokingly to James, "Can't we get a detection system as good as that? We keep having breakdowns and minor collisions because the whole railway system's starved of investment." James telexed us and we got in touch with Parrivale. Their system is excellent. Rather than let British Rail—a state system—contact another state system, we got in between. It's supposed to be a merchant banker's expertise nowadays; to get between the paper and the wall, or something like that.'

He grinned broadly. 'That's right. And I've been told the system is very good. But to be fair, it was your finance package that did it; I mean, the Brazilians have no money at all for external purchases of that sort. In a way you pioneered a new sort of counter-trade deal.'

'Well, not really. Everyone hates counter-trade because it isn't like a nice clean payment or even a long-term credit. The Brazilians were insisting on a mixture of counter- purchase, that is, taking exports in part-payment, and offset. By offset they wanted thirty per cent equivalent investment in Brazil. As it happens, we handle substantial timber exports from Brazil as well as other commodities so that covered the counter-purchase bit. White's do Brasil—that's our São Paulo friends and relatives—happens to be swimming in unremittable profits so we got the client to agree to a term loan rather than a proper offset. Altogether it worked out very well for all concerned. Parrivale got paid here by us on shipment; we got good deals on timber and finance; the

34

Brazilians got their signalling system. We pipped a couple of clearing banks at the post, too.' As it happened, it had been a deal, regarded with deep suspicion by Jeremy, that had cheered me up considerably, particularly in view of my doubts about my profession. Casey was nodding with interest and agreement as I spoke but he put up one more question.

'What about local manufacture content?'

'That was a problem. The Brazilians insisted on an element of local manufacture, as they usually do. The way in which that was handled and the means of remitting royalties and payments for know-how are, shall we say, one of the low-profile aspects of the package.'

His eyes met mine and he smiled again, faintly. My meaning was not at all lost on him. There were aspects, shall we say, that were not illegal but we would not like them publicized; it was also clear that I wasn't going to tell him any more; he'd bloody well have to pay for the next part.

He looked at his hands. 'You've been very forthright. I appreciate that. My bank has clients—two in particular— who are very keen to get involved in similar arrangements for the export of equipment to Brazil, also connected with railroads but not, I believe, competitive with your client or likely to cause a conflict of interest.' He looked up at us, first me, then Jeremy, a clear, professional eye-contact look.

'Would you be interested, you and your associates in Brazil, in putting together another similar package, for a similar type of deal? With us, on an agreed basis?'

Jeremy looked at me blandly and then at Casey. 'Of course. In principle, of course we would be interested; it's our business.'

'Fine. In that case, having obtained your agreement in principle, I will contact my side again and come back to you with details for discussion. Perhaps in the meantime you'd be good enough to decide on what basis

35

you would wish to be involved. Does that seem to be in order?'

Jeremy raised his eyebrows; I could tell he was slightly disappointed at getting no further. 'How long are you going to be in London?'

'Oh, several days more. I have a few matters to work through with the clearing banks I mentioned. I'm staying at the Hilton.'

'My dear chap! In that case why don't you join us for dinner one evening? Tomorrow's out but what about later in the week? Friday evening? It'll be purely social but we can decide where to take things from there. I'm sure that your own countrymen will be wining and dining you but it'll make a change, perhaps, to mix with the natives?'

'Why—why, that's very kind. I'd like that.' 'Splendid. Tim, you'll come too? With Sue? 'Great.'

With due ceremony and careful courtesy, the American departed. Jeremy shut the door, went to his desk, sat down, blew heavily and looked at me.

'Now what d'you suppose that was all about? Don't scowl so, Tim, there's a good fellow. You look quite congested.'

'Load of codswallop. The Americans are perfectly capable of doing their own counter-trading. First Boston are up to their necks in it. Yanks are a load of jealous gentlemen; they don't give business to foreigners if they can help it. I think he was just trying to pick our brains.'

'I liked him. And James introduced him. He seemed very straight to me.'

'I must say that I was a bit surprised that you invited him to dinner. Liked the cut of his gybe, did you?'

'Oh really, Tim! Leave off the yachting puns! Yes, I did; but a dinner'll maybe open him out. And I'd like Mary to have a look at him; always useful.'

The City is traditionally supposed to be about swift judgements on men, the quick eye of the experienced bird shot. Jeremy considered himself no different, despite the advent of computers. He gave me a hopeful look across the desk. 'We are lunching together today, aren't we, Tim?'

'Sorry, Jeremy. I'm tied up today.'

'Oh no! My dear Tim! You don't mean that I've got to have lunch in the dining-room with all those depressing people?'

'If you are referring to our co-directors and our clients, Jeremy, yes.'

His lip pouted. 'I'm not having it. I shall go to eat with my friends in insurance. We may need them soon.'

'Accident or fire?'

He didn't reply; one look was quite sufficient.

CHAPTER 6

There's not much left of Whistler's Chelsea. The village on the banks of the Thames, with its separate identity and historic connections, was rudely swept into London as far back as 1874, when they pushed the grand Embankment through, isolating the village from the muddy riverbank shores that once lapped its houses and pubs. Not many yards of concrete, asphalt and stone separate the village from the river—perhaps twenty—but they're enough; enough to alter it irrevocably in character from a fisher-port to a roadside jumble of church terraces blurred by the thunder of heavy traffic, engine fumes and ill-tempered bridge-crossers. You can't discern the houses that were once separate and stately from the road; there's pleasant architecture and good trees, fine windows and careful gardens, but they're close together, London-bound. If you wander down Tite Street for a change of architecture, to look at the studios and the bright red brick, the terracotta sunflowers of 1870s Queen Anne, you won't find the White House that E. W. Godwin designed for Whistler; a bomb obliterated it in 1940.

Oscar Wilde's house is still there but he wasn't much luckier than Whistler, for all his interior by Godwin; bankruptcy forced him out, too. Cremorne House and gardens, beloved haunt of Whistler for the firework displays, the dancing and the Tivoli-type ladies of easy virtue, were razed and built over soon after the Embankment arrived. The fields that separated Chelsea from London have disappeared; the old houses and quaint shops that Whistler painted were probably used as hard core for the Cadogan-Sloane estates, who evicted thousands of Chelsea residents from their cottages in 1909 and 1926 to build flats.

I bought Sue a pub lunch at the King's Head. It put me in a pleasant temper. You can't object to a pub like that even if it does sometimes attract the wrong people;

38

all pubs do from time to time. After all, it is old, genuinely old, and there's no bogus red plush. A good range of bitters and game pies; what more do you want? I ate a pickled onion with satisfaction, ignoring Sue's meaning look as she sipped her white wine primly. I decided it wouldn't be tactful to order another bitter, even though we weren't expected until two.

'I suppose he must have come in here,' I said, looking round at the polished glasses, the old window-frames.

'Whistler? I suppose so. Don't think of him as an alehouse man, though, do you? Too fastidious. Besides, an alehouse keeper would have wanted paying. Whistler preferred to entertain on tick in his own lofty rooms in Lindsey Row, dispensing his literary breakfasts at lunch-time, especially on Sundays. Quipping with Rossetti and Swinburne was more his style once he came over from Paris; this place and Cremorne would be for Charles Augustus Howell and similar shady dealers with their tarts.'

I gave her a sly glance. 'Whistler wasn't above tarts, particularly not Howell's. What about his portrait of Rosa Corder?'

She pursed her lips. 'You have a coarse mind, Tim. You can never think of art without some prurient reference or another.'

'Well, it's not surprising, is it? I don't work in a museum. Not that a museum's any restraint, of course. Look at Mortimer Wheeler; turned the British Museum into a private harem, by all accounts.'

She put her tongue out at me. It emphasized the moist generosity of her mouth and I beamed so broadly that she blushed and dropped her eyes. I took her hand.

'You're a smashing bit of fluff. Why don't we forget Harwell and—.'

'Tim! You're working and so am I! Now finish your drink and let's go. It won't matter if we're a bit early.'

I sighed. 'Very good, ma'am. On our way. Come on, it's just round the corner.'

We left the pub and I put my arm round her as we strolled back along the Embankment and crossed Oakley Street. At Cadogan Walk, before Flood Street, I turned her into the late Victorian stretch that ran at right-angles to the river, and we walked up to our destination. It was a late, grey-brick terrace of three-storey houses, encrusted with fancy mouldings around the lower bay windows; not a particularly 'Chelsea' image. Each unit consisted of a front door above a flight of stone steps, a bay window to the right of the door, a sunken cellar window below and a stretch of plain sash windows, two by two, above. A single attic window dormered the standard slated roof sloping down to the gutters. Plain London housing of the late nineteenth century, for plain London Pooters, with lots of stairs to trudge up and down inside. I opened the gate to the short front garden and we walked up the brief path, tiled diagonally in shiny-red glaze, to the stone steps. At the top I pressed the white button of the electric bell set in a circular metal holder to the right of the glazed'upper door panels. Sue cocked her head interestedly at the original stained glass in the two long rectangles above the solid lower half.

The door opened. No surprises. Mr Harwell was gentle, old, Pooterish, grey-trousered and brown-cardiganed. Shiny spectacles glinted on the clean pink face below wispy white hair. He wore a collar and tie and smiled pleasantly in inquiry as he cocked his glasses at us. I noticed that his black shoes were spotless.

'Mr Harwell?'

'Yes?'

'I'm Tim Simpson of White's. I'm afraid that we're a little early. This is my—er—colleague, Sue Westerman.'

His smile became more kindly. 'Of course.' He held his hand out to Sue, shook hands, did the same to me. 'Do come in. I'll lead the way.'

Big surprise.

It was a shock. The dull conventional exterior gave no hint of it. Beyond the inner hall door, out of sight, a fantasy-land smacked the eye with astounding colour, glitter and extravagance. Sue gasped out loud, to the well-anticipated pleasure of old Harwell. He beamed at us, waiting for the reaction.

It was astounding. The walls were washed in an off-white, brilliant background on to which a hand-applied pattern of gold-painted, tadpole-like curlicues had been added. The carpet stretched deep-red to and around the flight of stairs, which had lost its conventional square-tread rectangularity due to the application, on each and every step, of Rococo shaped mouldings which arched the back of each tread, leaving only the centre clear. The whole lot was picked out in gold and white, starting at the eye like a Jacob's ladder from- a Hollywood musical of the nineteen-thirties. The banisters were re-plastered with decorated mouldings picked out in gold. At the turn of the stairs wildly-ornamented gilt-framed mirrors, carefully angled, reflected the gold-commaed walls, the lavish staircase, the red-plush hall. To my left, on the wall, another madly exuberant gilt mirror revealed my open mouth, Sue's arched eyebrows and Mr Harwell's delighted smile.

'Surprised?' he inquired gently.

My throat was dry. 'Amazing. Er—extraordinary. Quite superb.' I peered more closely at the fantastic gold smears on the white walls to find that each shape had been applied by a finger, not a brush. 'Is it all hand done?'

'Oh yes.' His voice had all the satisfaction of the contented do-it-yourself handyman. 'My brother and I did it all. By hand.'

'Mr Harwell!' Sue's voice had taken on the rich admiring tone I knew she used for buttering up old males. 'It is *beautiful!* Absolutely wonderful! And you did it all yourselves?'

He nodded, glowing.

41

'Oh yes. My brother and I have spent years on it. I'll show you it all, if you like.'

'Oh yes! How marvellous! I wouldn't miss it for anything!' I gave her a glance but it bounced off, like stone. She clustered round the old man as would a crowd of admirers.

'This is just the hall,' he chirruped, unnecessarily. 'I'll show you the downstairs sitting-room first.'

Turning to the right, he opened the door of the front room, the bay-windowed net-curtained traditional front parlour, and we went in to an Aladdin's cave. I'm not sure that I didn't say Jesus Christ out loud because Sue gave me a quick disapproving look despite the fact that her mouth was open.

'Good gracious,' she managed to croak.

The wall decoration was the same again; gold and white but this time with red interspottings between the curled motifs. I could see that the separate gilt curls were less tadpole-like, more varied in shape and colour, browner in hue than the ones in the hall.

'The Autumn Room,' said Harwell, stiff with pride. 'You see the falling leaves all over the walls?'

I swallowed. It wasn't only the falling leaves I had to cope with as they fell gaudily from under the high picture rail, picked out in gold. Nor was it only the moulded plaster ceiling on which the roses, the corner-moulded acanthus leaves and the other decoration had been smeared with waxy gilt. It was the ruddy Staffordshire all over the place. On every blasted piece of over-decorated, cheap, flimsy Victorian furniture, smothered in meretricious ornament of the sort that drove the followers of William Morris mad, on every shelf, mantel, surface, bracket and corner except the actual seats of the bendy cabriole-legged chairs and settee were Staffordshire ornaments of the kind that initially sent me reeling. Dogs, King Charles spaniels, children, women, Victoria, Albert, generals, reformers, politicians—Gladstone glared at me pop-eyed—lovers, enemies and animals cluttered the scene. I scowled at them balefully. It was like a fairground stall gone mad. Harwell gazed at them fondly.

'Marvellous, aren't they? I sometimes think our country's real greatness is represented by the best of Staffordshire, don't you?'

I swallowed again. My eyes began to re-focus after their initial shock. As I began to take it all in, to become accustomed to the light from the netted bay window, I suddenly caught sight, among all those garish figures, of some earlier Staffordshire. A Prattware jug—the Sailor's Farewell. A pretty figure of a girl with a lute. An idealized gardener leaning on a spade with a basket of fruit beside him. A Whielden tea-caddy. Peeping out from behind Victoria and Albert, a glazed cow-creamer. Two sheep with bocage behind. A bird. A figure of a man—

'That's Ralph Wood,' I said, startled, stabbing my finger at it.

'Oh yes,' Mr Harwell agreed emphatically. 'Definitely Ralph Wood.'

Sue's eyes met mine, wide and shell-shocked. This was a Good Move after all, I thought to myself smugly, she'll never forget this. I gave her a synthetically warm smile in front of Harwell.

'Amazing, eh, Sue? Quite the most extraordinary collection of Staffordshire that I have ever seen. You and your brother must be very proud of it, Mr Harwell?'

'Oh yes. It is probably the finest collection in private hands today, you see.'

'Indeed? Well, it is tremendous. Tremendous. You have some very good early pieces, eighteenth-century ones.' Amongst the rubbish, I thought to myself.

'Oh yes. My brother is particularly a connoisseur of early Staffordshire, you see.'

'And the room. Amazing.'

'Yes. Well, I think we can safely say that this is one of your smaller stately homes, you see.'

There was a brief silence. Sue's face didn't move a muscle.

'Would you like to come upstairs? The main sitting-room — the one we use for everyday — is on the first floor.'

'Of course. We'd love to.' Sue smiled brilliantly. 'Is your brother in, too?'

'Oh no. He is away now, you see.' He led the way up the incredible staircase, turning at the top on to the first-floor landing, which was decorated just like the hail. Pausing for a dramatic moment he waited until we had joined him and then he threw the door open.

The room went right across the middle of the house, about twenty to twenty-four feet, taking in the two sash windows of the façade. It was high-ceilinged, with mouldings which had been left white, but the rest of the ceiling surface was deep dark blue, spangled with silver stars. A dark blue-and-white flock wallpaper covered the walls surrounding the dark blue carpet. The furniture was all gilt-painted with blue velvet coverings. Sue let out a strangled noise. I stared speechlessly at the ceiling-sky above me, recognized an arrangement in stars of the Plough, or Charles's Wain if you prefer it.

'The Nocturne Room,' Mr Harwell announced proudly. I stepped carefully across the impeccable blue carpet towards the windows, trying to take it all in. My eye caught a large painting on the wall over the central fireplace. It was a vast Victorian job in a huge gilt frame, depicting a small child, a girl, sitting by a fireside with a Landseer-like dog of shaggy and enormous size peering at her. On the floor in front of her was a doll with an arm missing, on the carpet. A tear could be seen clearly on the sickly-sweet infant's cheek. A slight carpet-tremor of suppressed shudder came to me from Sue as she caught sight of it.

'My brother suffers from a bad chest,' Mr Harwell explained sadly. 'He has to stay at the seaside on doctor's orders, you see. We have been unfortunate as a family, I'm afraid. My sister suffers from a chronically weak heart; she's upstairs in bed now, being mostly bedridden. When my brother and I realized she was unlikely to lead much of an active life any more we decided we'd make the inside of this house—it's been our family house since it was built—as cheerful and interesting for her as we could. So we decorated it ourselves. So that she could look at beautiful things all the time.'

'Good gracious.' Sue's voice was full of warmth and sympathy. 'How distressing, but what a wonderful thing to do for your sister. She must be absolutely delighted with it. And very grateful to you.'

Harwell smiled broadly. 'Yes, it is nice for her. She can still come downstairs with assistance but she's very weak. It started as angina but it seems to have got worse.'

I stuck my hands in my pockets. 'What a labour of love, Mr Harwell. It must have been an enormous effort, after work, to do all this and, indeed, the cost—? Quite a strain, I imagine.'

He gave me a composed stare. 'Oh, we retired a while ago. We were in the Trade, you see, and there was no one to carry the business on, so—'

—So that's how you put it all together, I thought. No wonder; tax deductible gilt paint.

Sue was still all womanly sympathy. 'No one to carry on? You never—I mean you or your brother or sister never had any family?'

'No. Oh no. We were all very close, you see. Always lived together. Happy with each other, you see. We were very upset when my brother had to think of his health. But we still see him from time to time, of course. He's well settled and much better.'

Family recitations are not my line. I tried to get a grip on things. We didn't have all day to come to the point of our visit.

'Mr Harwell, you called this the Nocturne Room. Was that because—'

'Of Whistler? Oh yes. It was the Peacock Room that inspired us, you see. Particularly downstairs.'

Sue caught my eye. 'You mean the room he decorated for the Leylands in Queens Gate? All gilt and blue peacocks?'

He nodded vigorously. 'Wonderful! Wonderful! We've got pictures of it. The Leylands treated him dreadfully! They had no right! To ban him like that—dreadful! And the room is in America now. Lost forever.' Real emotion stirred his gentle features; America might be the lost continent of Atlantis from his expression.

Sue agreed with him gently. 'In the Freer Gallery. Shipped over lock, stock and barrel.'

'Peacocks are supposed to be unlucky,' I said out loud. 'Is that why you haven't used them?'

Dreadful treatment? I was thinking to myself. Surely not. Whistler deserved what he got. Talk about biting the hand that fed him! Leyland was a generous patron and Whistler insulted him unforgivably, apart from getting a bit keen on his wife. If I'd been Leyland, Whistler would have got a broken nose as well as a ban from entering my household.

Harwell blinked at me. 'I—er——we hadn't really thought about it that way. I think we just thought that it'd be too hard for us to do. I mean, we couldn't be Whistler's standard, could we? He was superb, a master of artists, wasn't he? Absolutely on his own; one of the greatest painters ever.'

'Um, well, yes, I suppose many would agree. Talking of Whistler now, Mr Harwell, I wonder if we might—'

'Of course! Of course! Forgive me for carrying on so! Let me show you the items for sale.'

Sue and I stared at each other in suspense. I could hardly believe it. Was this extraordinary house about to disgorge a genuine Whistler? What did he mean—

'items'? More than one of them? There had been enough surprises already; I braced myself for the final moment.

Harwell twittered across to a gilt writing-table and slid open a drawer. My heart sank; surely the painting wouldn't be in there? He reached inside and pulled out two ordinary instamatic photographs, colour prints of the sort families take at Christmas.

'I'm sorry about the photographs,' he smiled, 'but I think you'll be able to get a good idea from them. I am acting in absolute confidence, you see; the paintings are for sale to the right type of party, but I have to be very careful. They are in safe keeping until we find a suitable buyer who is genuinely interested.'

So he was no fool. I smiled to myself as I took the first photo, still taken aback. Two photographs; surely not two Whistlers? He handed the other to Sue, who was standing beside me to look over my shoulder and we both grunted out loud.

Mine was a river scene. A busy river scene. Docks in the background were to be seen through a tangle of ships' rigging and congested river traffic. In the near-right foreground sat a man and a woman, slouching in chairs on what appeared to be a balcony, from which the scene had been painted.

'Wapping,' said Sue; a single, sharp, excited word. 'Definitely Wapping. Another version, though; slightly different angle. Never seen this one before.'

I gave her a cautionary look. I didn't want her to sound too excited; it would put the price up. The painting was half-familiar to me, even though Whistler's known painting of Wapping went to America at an early date. This was slightly different, as she had said, but still recognizable, with the long bend of river giving shape to the mess of barges, sails, steam tugs and stately three-masters huddled together. I guessed that the woman was Jo Hiffernan, but the man was a stranger, bearded, perhaps a temporary model. If this was genuine, it was a major find.

The other painting was a portrait. An elegant woman in a long dress of the eighteen-seventies, standing hand on hip, holding a muff.

'Maud,' Sue and I chorused together. 'Definitely Maud Franklin.'

'Mr Harwell,' I said quickly, looking up from the slides. 'I—,

The front doorbell rang, cutting me off in mid-stream. Blast, I thought, blast, just when things were getting really exciting. Instinctively I glanced out of the window, through the net curtains. A grey Jaguar saloon that had seen better days was parked across the road, engine running. A tight-packed sort of bloke sat at the wheel, smoking. I couldn't see who was at the front door; he was vertically below me.

'Oh dear,' Mr Harwell said. 'Please excuse me; that's the front door. I wasn't expecting anyone. I won't be a moment.'

He buzzed off downstairs, leaving me and Sue staring at each other. Her eyes were glowing and her whole complexion was pink and excited.

'Oh Tim! How exciting! And what a sweet old man. Do you do this sort of thing all the time, you lucky old trout? Have these sorts of visits?'

'Of course. Happens repeatedly. Mind you, I only take my favourite mistresses to them. Like Whistler. Gives 'em no end of a tickle.'

'Bastard.'

We heard voices downstairs as Harwell let in whoever it was and they transferred themselves across the hall into the first sitting-room, among the Staffordshire pottery. Voices started to float upwards, indistinct to begin with. I looked at the sentimental Victorian child with her dog and broken doll with a grimace. Sue followed my gaze and wrinkled her nose. The voices continued, one clearly Harwell's, the other unidentifiable. Then we heard Harwell's much clearer, more high-pitched.

'Oh no! Please don't do that! Please!'

Sue's eyebrows arched at me. A furrow quickened between them.

'Where, then?' The other voice was raised too, in a deeper London twang.

The reply was lower, less distinct. Then it came: the clear sharp snapping of a piece of pottery breaking.

'Oh no! Oh dear! No!' Harwell's voice was high, frightened, full of distress. 'Not that one! Please!'

Smash! Another horribly distinct breakage, with a tinkle of pieces. I flashed a look at Sue. I knew my own instincts, but I'd promised, I'd faithfully promised.

Her eyes glared at me furiously. Well, don't just stand there, they said, for Christ's sake *do* something, man.

'Stay here,' I hissed at her.

Thank God, I thought, as I scudded quietly down the landing and tripped down the ridiculous ornamental staircase, thank God she was here and she couldn't possibly object to this; no one could.

At the downstairs sitting-room doorway I stopped to take a quick shufti. Old Harwell was facing the door but he was so distressed, so frightened and tearful that he didn't see me. Facing Harwell, with his back to me, was a medium-built individual with short dark hair, in a sports jacket and stained cords. On the floor beside him were scattered the smashed pieces of a Victoria and Albert figure-pair and what I took to be the remains of a King Charles spaniel. Harwell was crying openly. The stranger picked up a Prattware jug in his left hand.

'Movin' up the scale,' he said with relish. 'Nah then, where is it? All we want is a fair chance at it, see?' He lifted the jug up to the level of his shoulder, arm outstretched. 'Ere we go, then. Last time: where is it? I've got all day and you've got a lot to break.'

I like Prattware. 'Don't drop that,' I said, stepping across the room.

There was no time for him to turn enough as I grasped his wrist, twisted it and locked his arm across me; I wrapped my other arm round his neck. My lips were close to his left ear as I braced his head hard back. He let out a choked squawk, strangled because I'd pinned him tight and had an arm round his throat. I bent the locked arm back at the elbow joint, the wrong way. He gave a gasp of pain.

'First the jug. If you drop it, it'll cost you two hundred as well as a broken arm and the price of the other two. So you just release your fingers, gently, as Mr Harwell here takes the jug off you then we'll find out what you're up to, eh?'

His reply was unprintable.

I tightened the grip on his neck, turned the wrist and put real backward pressure on the strained elbow joint. He gave a terrific high-pitched scream of pure agony and went rigid.

My lips were still close to his ear. 'Have you ever seen anyone with his arm broken backwards at the elbow, chummy? I'll tell you something; I have and it's bloody painful. Happened to a pal of mine during the Leicester match. I'll tell you something else; the quacks never get it quite right again 'cos it's a tricky joint to smash. Now then, Mr Harwell; you just take the jug, eh?'

The old boy darted forward and retrieved it, gasping with distress. I kept the stranger locked tight.

'Who is this? What does he want?'

Harwell shook his head. 'Oh dear! I—I can't—this is awful—my pottery—look at it—oh God—please—please go—' Incoherently he wept and bobbed his head with emotion.

'OK. Perhaps chummy and I had better talk outside to avoid any further damage. Open the front door, would you, please?'

Harwell managed 'that. He shot across the room into the hail and I heard the door being opened. Keeping the Staffordshire-smasher locked tight, I marched him across the room, down the hall, past Harwell and out on to the doorstep.

'Let go of me,' he snarled between teeth clenched with pain.

'Certainly.'

As I propelled him off the top step, releasing the arm, I took the precaution of hooking my left foot behind his ankle and giving a quick yank. He sailed down the five stone steps tangle-legged and landed with a satisfying smack prone on the red encaustic tiles of the short front path.

'Now then,' I said genially, starting forward, 'what's all this about, eh?'

The door of the tatty grey Jaguar saloon across the road flew open and the hard-packed bloke emerged, hurling away his cigarette. He shot across the asphalt and came up the path in a charge, chin tucked down. As I got the first full view of him I recognized a squaddie, or an ex-squaddie. No mistaking the type; short hair, tight flesh, bunched muscle, big shoes, no fashions, probably tattooed. A soldier. It wasn't the right time to speculate much, though; his heavy rush was going to take a bit to stop and I thanked my lucky stars that I was still at the top of the stone stairs. His legs looked powerful inside his cords and he had a fast sprint; I didn't like the look of him, not at all.

As he got to the third step I leant back a bit, transferred my weight on to my left leg and brought the right up in a punt-kick into his solar plexus. There was some skill in this; you can't kick from dead in front because the target will grab your leg and overrun you, absorb the blow, push you over backwards and kick the life out of you. You have to swerve sideways like a matador and bring your foot into its objective from a difficult side-angle.

Mine wasn't half a bad effort for a man supposed to have become soft with City living; quite accurate it was, about three inches below the fork in the ribs and curving upwards at the maximum velocity. Even so, it nearly knocked me off my feet; luckily the front doorway was behind me so I used it as a back-stop.

He knelt down thoughtfully on the top step, crouching on all fours, winded but close to me. His mouth worked to try and pump air. His eyes bulged.

'Don't get up,' I advised him cheerfully. 'Better to stay double for a bit.'

He launched himself at me like a battering-ram, still crouched. Side-stepping, I guided his head into the doorjamb with a satisfying thud. Stunned, he paused to think seriously for a while, still on all fours. His pal began to pick himself up from the tiled path.

'Tim!' Sue's voice was high, strained, almost as much a shout as a query. I turned to look inside the house in a reflex action, thinking that a third party had joined the mêlée. I had just enough time to see her querying face on the plaster-garlanded stairs before the squaddie, still on all fours, hooked my right leg with his arm, throwing me off my balance. As I went over sideways I realized for the first time that the stone stairs to the front door had no rail to them, evidently not being considered high enough. Four or five feet isn't very far to fall if you go over the edge of such steps but there can be snags and one made itself evident right away. The sub-basement window below the bay was cut into the ground with a concrete-lined well around it which went round as far as the steps to allow light to get in. It increased the fall into a hard, cramped space by another three or four feet. Just enough for me to have a hell of a job landing without breaking wrists and ankles or smacking hard-headed against the concrete.

By the time I'd extricated myself, bruised and limping, the two men had scarpered down the path, leapt into the Jag and burned off with screaming tyres. Sue gratifyingly rushed out on to the steps in alarm to find me but I did have to reflect, as the Jag disappeared, that it is at such moments that women do rather get in the way.

CHAPTER 7

She turned back from the window overlooking the gardens and sat down on the easy chair beside the long glass doors so that she could look out. After a sip or two from the cup of tea on the table beside her she put the cup down, picked the teaspoon up from the saucer and began to tap the side of the cup with it. After about five taps she looked up, caughtmy eye and quickly put the spoon back in the saucer.

'It's no good,' she said, looking straight at me.

'What isn't?'

'You.'

We were back in Onslow Gardens. Attempts to calm old Mr Harwell down, to get him to explain, had been fruitless. He was distraught, emotional, no: terrified. We helped to pick up the distressing pieces of broken pottery despite his pleas that we needn't. Rage boiled in me. Whoever it was and whatever the reasons they had for this kind of intimidation, they knew their subject well. An old, gentle man, surrounded by his dearly-loved possessions. A helpless invalid sister upstairs. Interesting that Harwell himself hadn't been touched— yet. That spoke of professionalism, lack of evidence in an inquiry. Broken china can always be attributed to accidents; bruised and injured old people are harder to explain.

Harwell would tell us nothing. He gulped, evaded, shivered. Mention of calling the police made him worse to the point of panic. I hadn't had much time to consider the implications of that; he had been a dealer once, with his family, and many dealers have something to hide. You can't bully a frightened old man who's just been terrorized; Sue and I calmed him down as best we could, agreed that it was now no time to discuss our business, pressed him gently once more to tell us what it was all about and got no real answer.

'It's a family matter,' he quavered uncertainly. 'Family matter. Please, not just now. My sister: she mustn't be disturbed or frightened. This might do untold damage to her health. These people say that they are from his family.'

'Who? What family?'

He shook his head. 'I can't—not now.'

'Tomorrow, then,' I urged. 'Let me come back tomorrow. Please, Mr Harwell; I want to help you.'

It was the best deal I could get. We left after eliciting a promise from him that he would see me again the following morning, that he would lock the door and let no one in until I came back. No further progress could I make.

'What do you mean, me?' I demanded.

She shook her head sadly like a schoolteacher contemplating a hopeless case of misbehaviour at a mixed infants' school. 'You do it all the time. Can't keep out of trouble, can you?'

'Oh, that's great! That's very fair! What did you expect me to do? Stand there like a prize burke while nasty-man smashed the entire collection and killed the old josser from grief? Eh? Your face was plain enough; get on with it, Tim, do something, it said.'

'Calm down! Calm down. I'm only saying that it does seem extraordinary that whenever you get involved in finding some art work or other, this sort of dreadful violence breaks out.'

'It does not! I have bought many pieces at auction, from dealers and privately, without the slightest trouble. The Fund is full of them.'

'You're not denying that there have been a few less—er—harmonious involvements?'

'One or two; pure chance. Just like today. It happens.'

'To you.'

I glared at her. She turned her hands down in a deprecatory gesture. 'I'm not saying it's your fault, Tim, just that it happens. That's why I've had to make a decision.'

'What decision?'

She got up, put her cup on the tray on the table, put her hands behind her, walked up and down and turned to face me, slowly. I could have screamed.

'I am going to be involved.'

'What?'

'Tomorrow morning. I'm going to come with you. I'll take the morning off.'

'Now look, Sue, there's no need—'

'Yes, there is! I know what'll happen if I don't. There'll be more violence—no, don't speak—of some sort, there'll be dreadful consequences, you'll probably get involved with some appalling floosie and—'

'Floosie? *Floosie?* Sue, what sort of school was it you went to? Floosies don't exist any more you know, they went out in—'

'Tim! Don't interrupt! You know what I mean. You have no taste in these matters. No resistance to the most flagrant females.'

I couldn't help smiling at that. 'Like art gallery girls, you mean?'

She flushed. 'You know jolly well what I mean! If I don't keep with you, you'll go off all over again, getting into trouble. Admit it.'

'Certainly not. I shall simply talk quietly to old Harwell like a Dutch nephew and try to persuade him that the paintings are safest off with us. There's no reason to suppose that there'll be any involvement in any further mayhem. Or that any—floosies—are likely to occur. Or that the whole thing has somehow got something to do with me.'

'Of course it has! Will have.'

'Why?'

'You heard what he said—the intruder. We both heard it. "Where is it? Where is it?" he kept on repeating. It's something to do with the Whistlers. It's bound to be.'

'Not necessarily. "It" is not "them". And you heard what Harwell said. Something to do with his family. You have no idea what other things Harwell may be involved in. He was trade. The place is full of goodies. It could be anything.'

'No, it isn't, I know it. It's the Whistlers. With you there it's bound to be.'

'Female intuition?'

She lifted her nose. 'Call it what you like. I know it. And I'm going back with you.'

I chose my words carefully. 'In view of—um—past history and when we went to Willy Morton's together and in view of your conviction this time, is that wise? I mean, from what you say you may be in danger yourself.'

She compressed her lips. 'You've changed your tune since this morning, haven't you? It was all pure chance then. Well, I don't care. I'm coming. If I come, at least there's a fair chance that nothing more will happen.'

'And I'll be kept out of temptation?'

'That too.'

'Not safe on my own, am I? Falling for flocks of gaudy houris all the time.'

'Not falling for. Falling on.'

'Sue! You have nothing to justify such a dreadful accusation. You and I are settled, aren't we?'

She gave me a withering glance that said don't start that all over again, then her eyebrows lifted in an arch of Eureka-idea brilliance. 'Of course! Why didn't I think of it? You must phone Nobby Roberts, now.'

'Eh? Nobby? What on earth for?'

'It's obvious! Nobby's an old friend; he's in exactly the right position. That'll clear it all before our visit tomorrow. Come on, phone him up at Scotland Yard now.'

'Sue, just because Nobby is a big cheese in the Art Fraud Squad doesn't mean that he'll welcome a request to look into a minor squabble in an obscure Chelsea street, for heaven's sake. Nobby's only involved in the big-time stuff now.'

'Nonsense! It's connected with the Whistlers! I'm sure of it. Phone him up and tell him everything.'

'But old Harwell's absolutely off the idea of the police. You could tell that, surely?'

'Of course! That's why Nobby's the right man. It's a quiet, discreet word from a friend. You can tell Nobby to tread carefully.'

'He'll love that.'

'Tim! Don't be so negative! I'm determined to keep you out of trouble this time. If you don't phone him up now I'll never speak to you again! If you've put it all in front of Nobby Roberts no one can say that you haven't acted properly. It's very important.'

She's such a teacher-type, she really is. It must be the lectures she gives at the Tate that do it. And there's nothing of your sloppy ex-art student about Sue, all scarves and shawls and woolly stockings; she's keen on light tweeds, woven suits, smart blouses. Slightly demure but always controlled in appearance, looking as though everything is running to plan. A hard image to resist. I sighed in resignation.

She nodded at the phone. 'Come on, ring him up.'

'What about the Whistlers? If the Force get involved there's a fair chance that we'll have the Whistlers blown sky-high and no hope of being the first to get in on them. There'll be a mad scramble once the story gets out.'

'Tim, how could you? That poor old man and his poor old sister! It's your duty to do everything you can to protect them. It's just like you and your Bank to—to be all mercenary about getting your greedy hands on his paintings regardless of his safety.'

Her eyes flashed at me. Form 2b had made teacher cross. With a sigh I picked up the phone, dialled Scotland Yard and asked for Chief Inspector Roberts. They did their best to put me off and get me to speak to some underling but I shocked them by using the most powerful phrase a big organization like that can take.

'This is a personal call,' I said.

There was an embarrassed silence, then they put me straight through. He wasn't pleased; I usually phone him at home.

'Hello, Nobby? Tim here.'

'What do you want?'

'Charm, now, Nobby, charm. The watchword of the modern police force. Try not to sound so suspicious. I am about to do you a great favour. Official business.'

'Oh yes?'

I could visualize the sandy-ginger complexion setting into a fixed expression, the light-coloured eyes narrowing, the muscles tensing on the lean jaw. Quickly and briefly I sketched in the background to our visit to Chelsea, described Harwell, the incredible house and then the incident with the two visitors.

He let out a hollow groan. 'Don't tell me—you've killed one and maimed the other for life?'

'No, no, no. Nothing like that. They scarpered after a slight altercation.'

'So what are you phoning me for?'

'Really, Nobby! Because you are an old friend in a key position. Because we played rugby together. Because a potential art crime or money-with menaces job should be of vital interest to you when it is connected with the background I've given you. Particularly in view of previous experiences. Actually, because Sue insisted I call you; she obviously has an edgy feeling about this business.

'She did? Why is she edgy?'

'Because she feels that there may be more trouble in the offing and she said that I should put the whole thing in front of you—cards on the table—and try to keep out of it myself. She liked old Harwell, he's a gentle old man and she felt he should be protected.'

'She's a good girl, that. About the only sensible thing in your household, as it happens.'

'Thanks.' I caught a gesture from her. 'She sends her love by the way. How are Gillian and the kids?'

'For God's sake Tim; Cut it out! I'm up to my eyes in about twenty cases at present. Give her mine back and tell her we're all fine. I suppose it was sensible but this isn't my line of country and you know it. It's a job for the local Chelsea station. I'll put a buzzer out with them and let you know.'

'Ah, well, fine, I understand, but you see we didn't know anyone at your Chelsea branch and you know what local rozzers can be like. Suspicious stares, beetling brows, black boots, the lot. Particularly in view of old Harwell's reluctance to involve the police. Didn't want them stamping all over his hoggin.'

'Don't worry.' His voice was defensive. 'We'll be discreet at this stage. If he was in the trade they'll probably know him down there. I'll make a few inquiries, tell them what's happened and let you know.'

'Splendid. You see? I'm behaving like a responsible citizen, aren't I?'

There was no reply.

'Nobby? I've arranged to see him again tomorrow, so—

'So I'll be back to you as soon as I can. In the meantime don't touch anyone or anything. Right?'

'Yes, Nobby.'

'Jesus Christ knows what this is going to lead to.'

'Really, Nobby! I—'

He slammed the phone down. I grinned at Sue. 'Told you he wouldn't like it,' I said.

She looked very relieved. 'That doesn't matter. This time you've played the game by the book, reported everything, withheld nothing. If there's any more unpleasantness they can't say you didn't act correctly.'

'True.'

She smiled at me. She was still upset about poor old Harwell but she looked much happier now. The burden of responsibility had been shifted, the tension released. We were not alone in our knowledge. I took her hand and we sat together on the sofa facing the fireplace with my Clarkson Stanfield above it. At least, I thought, relieved, we hadn't had anything really violent or horrible occur, just a bit of unpleasantness. And she felt involved, involved with me, involved in something exciting and yet unknown. It had been a good decision to take her.

'I know what you're thinking,' she said.

'What?'

'Both his mistresses. The Wapping scene has Jo Hiffernan in it and the other painting is Maud Franklin. Two of the most important ladies in his life. Before Trixie Philip Godwin came along.'

'Indeed. If they're genuine Whistlers, they're pretty important stuff. The Wapping one particularly.'

'Oh Tim! How tremendous! Wouldn't it be incredible if they really were genuine! I wonder where they are?'

I shrugged. 'No idea. Old Harwell said that he was acting for someone. Very guarded, wasn't he?'

'Poor old man. With good reason.' She gave me a soft smile. 'It was lucky you were there, really.'

'Dear old Tim. Pug-ugly number one.'

She grinned. Her eyes flashed. It was still afternoon so we made some more tea, but I promised to take her out to dinner later on; it seemed to me that we were set for a very pleasant evening after all.

CHAPTER 8

When the alarm went at seven she was lying half-across me. It seemed a shame to move her but I rolled over and stamped the bell-button off with an accurate thump. She opened her eyes and smiled.

'Rotter,' she said, half in invitation.

'Wanton,' I answered, with a grin. But I got up. It was going to be an important morning, with Whistler on the menu as a main course. I was ahead of her into the bathroom and so, too, was in the kitchen first. By the time she was dressed and presentable, I had our frugal breakfast ready. I even put out her fibre for her and she bowed in mock approval as she sat down. There was a sparkle about her, a shine of anticipation for our return to Chelsea. I rubbed my hands briskly as I sat down to orange juice, white toast and marmalade and tea.

The doorbell rang.

Sue shot a startled glance at me. Apprehension filled her face. I gave her a reassuring shrug, a half-frown of puzzlement as I swallowed a mouthful of juice and got up.

The doorbell rang again and the knocker was hammered, several times.

'All right!' I called, out loud. 'I'm coming. No need to batter the door down.'

I don't know why I still acted so calmly. I knew it couldn't be good news; it never is at that hour. Perhaps I wanted to protect Sue, to delay the moment, preserve our happy unison for a moment longer.

It was Nobby Roberts.

The sandy hair was tousled. His clothes had been put on in a hurry and he hadn't shaved. The white Rover out in the street behind him, with its long, luminous orange-red stripe, struck a chill into my heart. This was official business. He blocked the rest of the view with his lean frame; his eyes, pinkish-red, fixed mine hard. His face was set.

61

'Nobby?'

'Harwell,' he grated at me. 'George Harwell. Cadogan Walk, Chelsea. Right?'

'Eh? Are you coming in or what?'

'Only while you and Sue get your coats.'

'Eh?'

He advanced across the threshold and swung the door behind him. 'Harwell. That's who it was. That you phoned me about yesterday afternoon?'

'Yes. Yes, that's him. Why?'

He ignored the question. 'So you and Sue were the couple, seen by neighbours, present during an altercation yesterday afternoon?' His finger stabbed at me. 'In fact you were directly involved. The description fits.'

'I told you. Yesterday. All about it. I told you. What the hell is the matter with you, Nobby? Why are you here at this godforsaken hour?'

He breathed out heavily through his nose, mouth compressed, before he spoke. His eyes were closed.

'George Harwell of Cadogan Walk, Chelsea, was found dead this morning. Murdered. Cause of death is yet to be established. Upstairs an elderly lady, apparently his sister, was also found dead. Probably heart attack. Chelsea station phoned me this morning, half an hour ago, because I raised your query yesterday.' He opened his eyes. 'I want you both to come with me.'

I'll never forget Sue's face. She sat immobile at the table, one hand by her cup, the other in her lap. Her eyes watched me. It wasn't an accusing look or a hard one, just a look of acceptance, as though my involvement had certified Harwell's fate, as though my visit had put the black spot on him as a fact of life. It was the worst look I've ever had; I'd rather she had been angry or hysterical. It was so unfair. Nobody broke the silence until the tension forced me to speak.

'I'm sorry, Sue. Very sorry.'

Her voice was a whisper. 'That poor old man. And his sister.'

Nobby stared at me accusingly. It made me feel very defensive on top of the shock. He didn't say anything, though; he just looked. I got my coat and helped Sue into hers. Then we went out to his official Rover without saying a word. It took us just five minutes to get to Cadogan Walk as the car twisted through the clear light of the early morning streets.

Outside the Harwells' house there was a smaller police car and a few loiterers. A uniformed copper stood talking to a sergeant at tie gate. It was a very quiet, unexcited scene, like you get some time after a traffic accident and the buzz has died away. We went up the tiled path and the stone steps into the hallway with Nobby in the lead. No one called or shouted or said much. I took Sue's arm but she disengaged gently as we entered the house. I felt numb; the garish gilt-white of the hallway made me close my eyes for a moment.

Nobby was greeted by a tall raincoated man with polished black shoes and thin dark hair. He smiled briefly at Nobby and called him Nobby, not Chief Inspector or Sir or anything like that. Nobby introduced him.

'Inspector Johnson,' he said. 'Sam Johnson, of Chelsea CID.'

Johnson shook hands with Sue first and then looked at me.

'I know you,' he said flatly, matter-of-fact, neutral in tone.

'Really?'

'I was a detective-sergeant at South Ken until a year ago. You and Nobby were involved in the murder of another dealer, in his shop. Blackwell, his name was; he was still working, though. Nobby solved the case, as I'm sure you know.'

He glanced at Nobby and then back at me again. I felt awkward. I didn't remember him, not at all. There was a slight implication that Nobby and I might be somehow connected in a discreditable way.

'I was moved to Chelsea when I got promoted,' Johnson said, almost irrelevantly.

'Do we have to go any further?' I was thinking of Sue.

'The body's still upstairs. One of you will do.'

I stepped forward. As I did so I caught a quick sight of the downstairs front room and stopped in shock. It looked as though a bomb had hit it. Nobby drew in his breath sharply and I heard Sue gasp. Then a piece of china crunched under my foot. It was all over the floor of the room and bits had spread into the hallway. I must have winced because Johnson looked at me sharply.

'Did you see this yesterday?'

I nodded and moved to the doorway to look fully at the scene. By no means all the pottery was broken despite the shattered impression given by the piles all over the carpet. Pieces still crowded the shelves but less thickly than before; my gaze swept round the assembly looking in vain for some of the things we had seen. I scanned the floor but Nobby shifted uneasily.

'I think we'd better go up,' he said. 'I'll get one of the men outside to stay with you, Sue. Let's get it over with.'

He beckoned outside and the uniformed sergeant came in. Sue was looking dreadful. I didn't like to think about her as we mounted the ridiculous gilt-rococo staircase and flinched past the angled gold mirrors on the corner, up to the landing. Johnson led the way and turned us in under the silver stars set in the dark blue sky-ceiling above.

'The Nocturne Room,' I murmured involuntarily, causing Johnson and Nobby to give me long stares.

He was lying in the fireplace, covered by a blanket. At least I assumed it was him but my attention was slammed upwards over the mantelpiece to where the big Victorian painting was slashed into tatters. It was as though terrible rage had been vented on it. Cut after cut had been sliced through, stripping it into triangles, stripes and splinters. Even the crossed pine of the stretcher-frame was visible behind the shredded canvas. The awful intelligence came to me that Harwell must have loved that sentimental Victorian monstrosity.

'I'm sorry about this,' said Johnson, breaking my dumbfounded silence, 'but I have to ask you to look.'

He drew back the blanket. Old Harwell's face appeared, top half first, the eyes closed. The blanket went back further and—

'Christ!' I almost shouted.

It doesn't matter how many photographs you've seen, how many horror movies, television blood-baths. Nothing can prepare you for the real thing. Old George Harwell's throat had been cut. The rest of the face seemed quite composed but below the jaw there was a dreadful line clogged with black, brown and red colouring which had blotted into the neat shirt and tie. I felt very shaky as a sudden weakness loosened my leg muscles.

'His throat's been cut,' I said unnecessarily, just to say something, to break the silence.

Johnson put the blanket back.

'You identify him, though? The Mr Harwell you saw yesterday?'

I nodded, feeling sickly fascination. Nobby was looking at Johnson in a professional way.

'Odd,' he said. 'The bleeding—'

'Probably not the cause of death,' Johnson interrupted. 'The Doc's been for a first look. Impact of a fall most likely, and simultaneous blow to the head. Went into the fireplace. Throat cut afterwards.' His face was set. 'He'd been knocked around, too. No question but that it's murder.'

'The sister,' I said. 'What about her? They didn't—'

He shook his head. 'No. The guess is that she may have had a severe emotional shock or fright but death was due to heart attack. All subject to confirmation, though.'

'God. How awful.'

'Were you in here yesterday? This room?'

'Yes.'

He nodded absently. 'We'll have to print you. Both of you. The milkman raised the alarm. The Harwells were strictly regular with their empties. They had one of those little clock things that tell the milkman how many pints today. They always put it out. It wasn't there this morning and he couldn't raise them. He knew them well and all about 1he old lady's condition. He got a uniformed officer to open up. You can see the rest.'

'Good God.'

He glanced around. 'I couldn't believe it. Not after your call last night, Nobby. Couldn't believe it.' He looked at me. 'We'll need a very detailed statement and a description.'

'Of course.' I turned across to the gilt writing-table with the drawer that had held the snaps of the Whistler paintings. It was open. 'They've gone. The photographs have gone. The ones he showed us of the Whistlers.'

Nobby stared at me silently. 'Don't touch anything,' Johnson said. 'We'll find what prints we can. There's a brother, apparently. We're trying to find his address.'

'He's at the seaside. I don't know where. For his health.'

Johnson absorbed this without expression. 'We'll find him. Let's go downstairs.'

We went out into the sunlight at the top of the five stone steps. Sue was standing on the tiled path and I walked carefully down to her. I had to sit down on the low garden wall that separated the front garden from next door. My vision seemed blurred.

'An odd thing,' Johnson said to Nobby, holding up a small polythene bag with a multi-sided silver coin in it. 'We found this on the floor beside the head. Close to the mouth, as though it had dropped from his teeth.'

'Fifty p.,' Nobby stared at the six-sided piece. He shook his head. 'Motive wasn't purely robbery, then. Left him with half a sov.'

I managed to stand up, close to Sue. Quite carefully and deliberately she reached out and took my hand in hers, squeezing it very slightly.

'I'm sorry,' I said to her, uselessly.

She gave my hand another squeeze.

'Well,' said Johnson briskly. 'I think we'd better go to the station and start getting it all down on paper. You all look as though you could do with a cup of tea.'

CHAPTER 9

'Drop it! For heaven's sake, Tim, drop it!' Jeremy did an agitated turn up and down his carpet. 'Just drop the whole thing!'

'I have. I'm just a bystander. The police have the inquiry in hand.'

'I meant the Whistler, too. Just forget it. Don't persist.'

'I'm not. I've told you: the police have it all in hand.'

He glared at me suspiciously. Then he held up a warning finger. 'Now look here, Tim; I know you from past experience. You're a persistent beggar. I absolutely forbid you to take part in any further search of any kind for this painting. Is that clear?'

'Absolutely. It's exactly what the police said.'

'Oh, did they? They had the same thought too, I suppose.'

'Maybe. So did Sue. Actually they were very good with her. Treated her like an adult, no "now then little woman" stuff, all very matter-of-fact. Nobby's always had a good word for Sue, of course. Came as a shock when she stiffened 'em both up.'

'What? What did she do?'

'She told Nobby and this Johnson chap that if they didn't find old Harwell's murderer or murderers she'd never speak to them again. Didn't affect Johnson much but Nobby was quite put out. We shall proceed in the normal way with every despatch, etc., etc., he said, very po-faced, but you could see he was rattled. Sue and Gillian are pretty close, like each other a lot, so he's a bit outflanked. Sue feels personally involved; she'd solve the thing herself if she could.'

Jeremy grinned broadly before he remembered himself and assumed a serious expression again. 'Well, that's as maybe. Them to their business and us to ours. I shall not discuss this again. We've enough on our plates as it is, what with this Brazilian affair and all the rest.'

'Yes, Jeremy.'

He gave me another suspicious stare. 'It's probably been a very good thing. I'm glad we're dropping Whistler.' His gaze became challenging. 'I've always thought we should go in for some Impressionists.'

I sighed wearily. 'Jeremy, *everyone* buys Impressionists. Everyone. The object of our Fund is to lead, not to follow. We've always agreed on that. Besides, one of our targets has been to set up a really first-rate Fund in British art, particularly of the last hundred years. I want to get a Munnings and a Burra and a Hockney and a Wyndham Lewis and a—'

'All right! All right! I agree! I know; I've always agreed to it. We'll drop the Impressionists. But for God's sake don't get involved in a wild goose chase for the Whistler. If it turns up, it turns up. I'm not having you haring after it like you have before.'

'Hares don't go on wild goose chases, Jeremy, you're mixing—'

'Tim! Don't be flippant! You know what I mean.'

I grinned at him. His large frame was stiffened erect in the centre of his carpet. His blond hair gleamed. He gave me an affectionate scowl.

'You're winding me up. Deliberately. I should have known.' Humour slackened the tall stance and, crossing to his big mahogany partner's desk with its bulbously gadrooned edge, he sat down. 'Come on; enough of that. To business. What are we going to do about Casey?'

Relaxing, I sat opposite him and crossed my legs. 'It depends on whether you think we can really do business with him or not.'

'Of course we can. I must say, Tim, you're frightfully cagey about him. I thought he was a very straight fellow. Good American stock: I liked him.'

'Jeremy, Americans are not just ex-colonists who think the same way as we do but happen to have been born abroad. It's a foreign country you know, and they are foreigners. Their culture is quite different. There was a time—Whistler's time—when American culture was still largely shaped by English forebears, but not now. Our original contribution is barely discernible in modern American culture. People used to make the same mistake about the Irish. This chap Casey is both remotely Irish and absolutely American; I do hope you're not making the usual mistake of thinking he's some sort of distant cousin. The Americans owe us nothing—quite the reverse, in fact—and they are fiercely competitive. If they can skin us alive in business, they will.'

'My dear Tim, I'm not as green as all that! Damn it, I've been to the States, you know!'

'Sailing against all those sporting New Englanders with clubs and country houses and tweedy wives. You might just as well have been on the Hamble or at Cowes.' There I go, I thought as I said it, contradicting myself already.

'Really! You make me sound like Uncle Richard! I think your South American youth has prejudiced you. Besides, it's high time the Bank started to forge some more positive links over there. We do lots of dealing, everybody does, with the American side but we haven't got any real tie-ups of any kind.'

'You mean you want to sub up the odd sixty million dollars for a half-share in a suitable American investment bank, like Jacob Rothschild did?'

He pursed his lips; his brow furrowed. 'Not quite. But don't think that I won't be quick to raise money if the right opportunity occurs. And I do want to do business with Casey if I can. So tell me, now: what should we do?'

I ran through the options with him, taking the Parrivale deal as a base. With Casey we would be most likely to be acting as consultants, for which we would charge a fee, but we would also be asked to participate as part-principals as well, taking Brazilian produce, putting up local finance, working out how to extract royalties, closing link after link until the chain held to the satisfaction of everyone. Jeremy enjoyed this; the smell of a big deal always excited him. The running of an everyday business, even a fast-moving, risk-taking business like dealing in securities, was boring to him. He had to be getting on, expanding, piling structure upon structure as he moved towards a distant, larger, more resounding goal.

We covered the likely discussions we would have with Casey and he sat back, satisfied. 'Splendid. That clarifies everything for me. Anything more we should talk about?'

'Nope. Anyway, I have to be off.' I stood up. 'Duty calls.'

'What? Where are you going?'

'To buy a painting.'

'Eh? Now look here, Tim—'

'Calm down, Jeremy, calm down. The Fund has excess cash floating in it. Some more investment is needed. It's all within my budget and I don't need authorization; it's not a Whistler.'

He glowered at me. 'What painting? Where is it?'

I tapped my nose with my index finger. 'In the rooms. Trust me, Jeremy; just trust me.'

He sighed heavily. 'If only I didn't know you so well,' he said sadly.

CHAPTER 10

'Lot thirty-six.' The auctioneer gave the assembled throng a quick glance over his half-moons before looking with satisfaction to his left, where a porter had placed the framed canvas on an easel. 'Self-portrait with nude model by Sir William Orpen. Signed and dated 1917, oil on canvas.'

The estimate in the catalogue was eight to ten thousand pounds. I glanced quickly in again at the small crowd herded around Christerby's upper gallery without entering or getting too close to the men loafing in the big double doorway at the back. From where I was standing in the broad hallway outside I could see all I needed to see and I had no desire to enter just then.

'Start at four thousand?' queried the grey-suited, middle-aged man, looking like a respectable preacher up on his lectern. I knew George Jarman from previous experience; he had quite a confidential way with an auction room, respectful but firm, keeping the trade from getting too stroppy and lighting a kindly eye on private punters with money. He couldn't see me now as I moved carefully away from the entrance, feigning interest in a secretaire bookcase parked against the wall.

'I have four thousand. Four thousand five hundred. Five thousand.'

The painting showed Orpen in a battledress jacket, the embodiment of the Official War Artist, standing at his easel with his back to you, painting with palette in hand. Reclining on a couch at a short distance from him, across the room, was the naked blonde figure of Yvonne Aubicq, one of the partners in his life from the time he went to France and Belgium in 1917 until 1928, when they parted.

'Six thousand. Seven. Eight. Eight thousand pounds. Against you on my left. Nine. At nine thousand pounds.'

She was a remarkable woman, Yvonne Aubicq. When Orpen left her he gave her his Rolls-Royce and his chauffeur, a chap called Grover. Yvonne married Grover and they lived in the south of France. He became a racing driver, using the name Grover-Williams, on Bugattis; they were quite a well-known pair in racing circles and she was devoted to him. During the Second World War they worked for the French Resistance but the Germans caught him and did him in, nastily, in a concentration camp. She was devastated. Afterwards she lived in a wooden chalet house Orpen had given her outside Paris and she used to come across to England in the 1960s to judge championship dogs at Cruft's. Scottish terriers were her speciality.

'Ten thousand pounds.' George Jarman's voice took on a note of content. Top of the estimate realized; Christerby's honour would be satisfied.

Orpen was dead by then, of course. Fifty-three years old, he was, when he died of drink in 1931 in his house in South Bolton Gardens, not so far from Sue and me, in the Onslows.

'Are you all done at ten thousand pounds? At ten thousand pounds, then. At—'

I moved across into the middle of the doorway, making sure that Jarman, with his gavel poised in the air and his gaze circulating the room, saw me quite clearly. I nodded at him.

'Eleven thousand.' He brought his gavel down carefully, shifting his glance from me to the middle of the room where the main body of the people sat neatly in rows. Over to my left I caught sight of Charles Massenaux, reclining gracefully against a satinwood commode, looking forward at George Jarman, his eyebrows slightly elevated.

'Twelve thousand.' Jarman raised his eyes to me and got the affirmative he wanted. 'Thirteen.' He looked back into the centre again, where I recognized the back of the head of Morris Goldsworth, a specialist Modern British

73

dealer and not a favourite of mine, as Charles had indicated. A couple of boys in the trade, standing close to me, gave me incurious glances.

'Fourteen thousand.' I nodded without hesitation. 'Fifteen. Fifteen thousand pounds.'

Without seeming at all interested or disconcerted, Charles Massenaux turned his head languidly away from the front, sweeping the room with studied unconcern until he reached me. His head stopped. I didn't move a muscle as I saw him pause ever so slightly, watching me with interest. He uncrossed his long, pin-striped legs.

'Sixteen thousand.' Jarman looked up from the centre briskly at me. 'Seventeen.' His head went back curiously to the centre again.

The clever thing Orpen had done was to put a large mirror on the wall between himself and Yvonne, or maybe it was there in the room anyway. Orpen had a thing about mirrors; if you go to the Tate you can see his painting of an earlier model, Emily Scobel, seated under a convex mirror reminiscent of Van Eyck's painting of the Arnolfinis. Then there's a well-known self-portrait in a tin helmet, *Ready to Start,* where he stands obliquely in front of a mirror so you can see the side of his face. The bottles are there already — wine, whisky, whatever — in front of the mirror so you get a portrait and a still life, a bottlescape, all in one.

'Eighteen thousand.' Jarman was looking back at me. 'Eighteen thousand pounds.' The tone was hopeful but it put the pressure in my direction, briefly, as I nodded. 'Nineteen. Nineteen thousand.'

There's another one of Orpen's when he was much older, a multi-reflection of himself, going back into infinity. This one, however, was much more subtle; you had a view of Orpen from the back, painting, as I've said, and another, in the mirror, from the front, showing his face clear of the side of the easel: narrow, smooth-haired, intent. He often put himself in his paintings.

'Twenty thousand pounds.' Jarman's voice took on a slightly different tone. A rustle ran through the crowd. Double the estimate. It's not that twenty thousand is a lot of money to pay for a painting these days, it isn't, but the trade loves to chat about how the auctioneers have made a cock-up of their estimates yet again.

I nodded. 'Twenty-two thousand,' said Jarman, quite cheerfully this time. Charles gave me another stare. His nostrils flared slightly and he pinched the end of his nose. A slight furrow appeared between his eyebrows. We were upsetting Charles, ever such a little bit.

'Twenty-four thousand.' Jarman looked up again. In the mirror, behind Orpen, was the reverse reflection of the blonde Yvonne, propped up on her couch, one knee drawn up, relaxed. She was twenty when Orpen met her and he fell for her like a ton of bricks. Because of the effect of light and shade the second, mirrored view of her was more impressionistic, partly concealed, very subtly conveyed by brilliantly-placed dabs of paint. Two nudes for the price of one, I thought, with a wry inward smile; admit it, though, Tim, you're emotionally involved in this one.

'It's against you at the back.' Jarman's voice gently prodded me. 'Twenty-six thousand pounds? Twenty-six.' He nodded approvingly. 'At twenty-six thousand?' The pressure was returned to Morris Goldsworth in the middle of the hall. 'The bid is at the back.'

She was so like the late Marianne Gray, American blonde of bittersweet experience, that it was uncanny. There were times when it was a painful effort to look at her: I suppose that one of the unpleasant lessons of age is that past actions and memories can never be blotted out no matter how irrevocably, how finally, you think they have been concealed and forgotten.

'Are you all done at twenty-six thousand?' Jarman raised his gavel. 'At twenty-six thousand pounds . . .' He paused; Morris had given up. Smack! Down came the gavel and Jarman gave me an approving stare, almost a nod of approbation. 'White's,' he said crisply to the clerk beside him, loud enough for everyone to hear. The clerk bobbed his head, entered the notes into his book and glanced at Jarman, who doubtless rang up the pleasant thought of another five thousand-odd quid into Christerby's coffers, but didn't show it. 'Lot thirty-seven?' he demanded, looking up expectantly.

As the porters took the Orpen off the easel and replaced it with the next lot — it was a Ruskin Spear of Hammersmith — there was a rustle of relief, coughing, scrapes of chairs. A few heads turned to look at me. I marked my catalogue nonchalantly and strolled away from the doorway to find my way barred by a reproachful Charles.

'Was there something I should have known?' he murmured sadly at me. 'Something I missed, perhaps?'

'Missed?'

'Now come on, Tim, don't be difficult. Tell your Uncle Charles, there's a good boy.'

I smiled at him. 'No reflection, Charles, if you'll forgive the pun. You were quite in order with the estimate in many ways. There've been a number of Orpens come up in the rooms lately and they've all been around six, eight thousand; nothing spectacular. He's been somewhat out of favour for years.'

'So? What's the catch?'

'You want to hear my lecture on Modern British Art?'

He inclined his graceful head as he shook it. 'No, Tim. I want to know why White's Fund bought that painting, at that price.' His finger stabbed at me. 'What I mean by that is that *you*, Tim Simpson, bought that painting, at that price.'

I grinned, then I ignored the flattery. 'The three great portraitists of the halcyon years of the Slade were Orpen, John and McEvoy. Any collection of twentieth-century British painting that purported to be representative of the best—and White's Fund has to be just that—should have a really good example of each.

We already have a Gus John; one of those idealized landscapes with Ida and Dorelia and the children all littered about in it. I don't like it. This is a really cracking Orpen, representative of his best stuff: a self-portrait, a double nude, an interior and a still life—did you look at the table by his easel, with paint and jars and bottles all over it?—rolled into one. It was worth every penny—Morris Goldsworth thought so too: he was the underbidder, wasn't he?'

'Yes.'

'Well, there you are. He's a damned sharp dealer in Modern British. He knows. Compared to a Camden Town Group or a Newlyn School of that quality, the Orpen was cheap. You'll see; it'll be a good investment for sure.'

He nodded slowly, like a man stacking away a bit of knowledge into a carefully-opened memory bank. 'You're probably right. I shall look at Orpens differently from now on.'

'And I've charged you nothing for the advice.'

He gave me a quizzical look. Morris Goldsworth came out of the central room accompanied by a well-suited, ponderous young man in his twenties, marking his catalogue. Goldsworth paused to speak to someone and while he did so his heavily-spectacled eye, sweeping with the care of a professional, caught sight of me. He stopped, cold, and kept a steady stare at me while talking. After a few moments his conversation ended and he gave a slight gesture to the young heavy with him. Goldsworth knew, now, that I was aware of his gaze and his expression became hostile as he spoke out of the corner of his mouth. I put his companion down as soft, probably public school, a hooray henry. He looked at me markedly as Goldsworth murmured, then the two of them moved away. Charles Massenaux took my arm thoughtfully.

'Made yourself unpopular with Morris again,' he whispered, close to my ear. 'Naughty Tim.'

77

'Bugger Morris.'

He gave me one of his distant smiles. 'Still, since you are a friend and you have set a record for us for an Orpen—' He broke off and a look of alarm crossed his face. 'I say, you haven't got an Orpen at home, have you?'

'Charles, really! Only a drawing. Are you accusing me of ramping up Orpens?'

'Sorry. It was just an evil thought. As I say, since you are a—a friend, so to speak, I thought perhaps, well, a word to the wise, Tim.'

'What's up?'

He glanced round quickly. 'Morris Goldsworth approached me yesterday. Apropos of our last conversation, it seems he's on the same warpath as you.'

I lowered my voice. 'A Whistler? Well, it's not surprising. He's in the right part of the trade, after all.'

'In his case he has a very keen buyer, apparently, American. Claims he's acting for a member of the family, a relation of some sort.'

'You know what Yanks are like. Always claiming distant connections. Wait a minute—a member of the family?'

'Yes. This must have been a Welsh branch, I think, because it was a name like Williams he said they were related to, by marriage or something.' He stopped. 'What's up? You've gone all rummy-looking. Are you all right? Not regretting the Orpen, are you?'

Around us the stately pillars at the foot of the staircase, framing the expensive clutter of the panelled hallway, with its labelled furniture and transient paintings, receded into pale distance as the blood-rush concentrated my stare into the suddenly-magnified features of his long pale face.

'Winans,' I said hoarsely.

'Eh?'

'Not Williams. Winans. That he was related to. The name must have been Winans. Wasn't it?'

He blinked. 'Come to think of it, yes, that does sound like it. Why? Is it important?'

'Railways.'

'What? Tim, are you all right? What are you going on about?'

'The Winanses, Charles, the Winanses! I don't suppose they ever teach you anything about real life in your business, do they? The Winans family were builders of locomotives and rolling stock. On the Moscow railway, for Whistler's father. My life seems to be nothing but railways and Whistlers these days.'

CHAPTER 11

Charlie Benson's shop stands well down the King's Road, past the fashionable stretch, almost as far as the World's End pub. South-west of it the lorries thunder down Cremorne Road to the Embankment; Charlie is in Chelsea proper, a few blocks north of the river. It's a big shop and isn't anything like the sort that have moved into the Fulham Road, further north, all soft grey carpets and a single spotlighted item of reconstituted mahogany card table with wheezed-in concertina action at five thousand. Charlie's is a genuine shambles of an antique-junk shop; the windows look like a cross between an old ironmonger's and a ship's chandlery in which nothing was ever polished. There's even a diver's helmet, green with oxide.

I pushed the glass door open and waited for the clumps of copper pans, brass kettles and pewter pots to stop clanging on the ends of their strings. Glass cabinets, grimed with age, contained lousy china, Gosse mementoes, toy soldiers and moulded 'thirties figures of naked ladies in green cloche hats. An elephant's foot-umbrella stand contained ivory walking sticks, infantry swords and what looked like an African witch-doctor's virginity remover. One marquetry repro clock leaned against the wall. The girl behind the glass counter filled with piles of flowery plates and chipped cups glanced up once and then went back to her crumpled copy of the *Sun*. I went across to the notice that said 'More Upstairs' and paused at the treads.

'Charlie in?' I asked, glancing curiously at the girl revealed on page three; her knockers were enormous.
She turned the paper over sharply and jerked her head upwards. 'He's doing his layout.'

Upstairs the furniture mixed Victorian deal with Art Deco plywood. I pushed past a carved lion-mask-dominated wardrobe that was undoubtedly destined for Germany and four bergère chairs with splintered caning.

80

Beyond an upended sofa there was a door, central to the wall. I opened it and walked in to what Charlie called The Chapel.

It was a big room, high-ceilinged, set back at right-angles to the line of shops and attached to Charlie's building by a tenuous short passage. He said that originally it had been a religious meeting-room or chapel, low Church of some sort, about forty feet long by twenty wide. The peaked ceiling was crossed by three large joist-beams to give a suitably religious effect below the rafters. Most of the room was taken up by a series of continuous table-surfaces about six feet wide, all round the walls, covered by one of the biggest model train layouts I had ever seen. Charlie was in the middle, bending over a smaller workbench; he had inserted a fine screwdriver into the depths of a model loco. The tiny tool looked like a toothpick in his vast hand as he turned and straightened up to see me, with black-bearded grin.

Charlie Benson's height matched my own: about six feet. His width was far greater. It wasn't just that he had a big stomach because somehow you expected that. It was the vast width of him, the bulk, the feeling of power as he moved, like a prize bull bulging with fat and muscle. He wore a sort of smock-pullover, badly stained, and great flapping brown corduroys above suede chukka boots. He could have taken on the best all-in wrestler and broken his adversary's neck with ease any time. No one wanted to tangle with Charlie.

'Tim! How are you? This is a rare pleasure. Slumming, I suppose, now you've left the Fulham Road for the cloisters of South Ken?'

'That's it, Charlie. Christ, you've been at work on the trains.'

He smiled with pleasure. Around him circled an extensive miniature landscape of embankments, green fields and forests. Cottages sat in water meadows filled with toy cattle. A waterfall splashed down its rocky

81

plastic path to an inevitable hidden pump which made the poor thing do it all again. Cars stood motionless in winding lanes with dotted white centre-lines and old-style road signs. Country stations, fixed in a timeless nostalgic era of train-heyday, displayed the old timber black-and-white names, the paling fences, the filled roof canopies and rustic benches outside dignified waiting-rooms that might form the backdrop to an Agatha Christie story set in the never-never village of Marple Parva. Milk churns were being unloaded from rustic lorries far remote in design from the juggernauts rumbling down Edith Grove and Cremorne Road, lorries that were human in scale and native to the country.

Through it all, cinder-tracked, signalled, banked, tunnelled and viaducted, ran the railway lines on sleepers, with their occasional caterpillar-trains, green or red or brown-and-cream. Some had black engines to pull them, some were livened in maroon or green. Close to Charlie was a vast control panel festooned with wires and blinking with tiny traffic lights controlled by a microprocessor. All that expertise, I thought, dedicated to preserving a model of the past.

'It's fantastic, Charlie. You ought to open it to the public.'

He shoved two fingers up in the air at me. 'Fuck the public. The public are too bloody stupid to appreciate a thing like this. Let 'em build their own.' He winked at me to show it was nothing personal. 'This is for me. The only bloody thing that keeps me sane nowadays, the way trade's going.'

I nodded in sympathy. 'No steady trade at all, is there?'

'Of course there isn't! Effing yanks and Germans and riff-raff wanting this thing one day and another the next. You can't rely on anything.'

Charlie's classic trade bleat, the resentment of a breed who had it much too easy years ago always made me smile inwardly. If you work in a street market you have to have what's selling on your stall; apples today, pears tomorrow, bananas on Saturday. And next week it may be parsnips.

'Art Deco's the big thing now,' I said. 'All New York's gone Art Deco.'

He leered at me. 'Too bloody expensive. I get mine from France. It's half the price there. Any case, New York's an Art Deco city so why do they want to buy here?'

'They'll buy anything if it's cheap' I said, thinking of the Bank.

'Well, you can forget Art Deco for the Yankee trade. What do you think of the Brighton Belle there? The Pullman?'

'Beautiful. I've always loved model trains.'

'Oh? Didn't know you'd ever 'ad them. What was yours? Hornby Dublo?'

I hesitated. 'No. We lived in South America then. My father got me a Lionel. American stuff was much easier to come by, somehow.'

'Pah!' He practically spat. 'Bloody Yankee stuff. Mind you, Hornby were always to blame. They let the Yanks and more especially the Germans -- Märklin, all those — take the bloody market from them. Stupid sods. They had—and still have—some of the best in the world. Could have beaten 'em into a cocked hat. Went bankrupt instead.'

'I always liked my Lionel,' I said mildly. 'You put a powder in the loco funnel and it used to puff smoke for you. Then there was a super level-crossing; every time the train went through a little bloke dashed out of the crossing- keeper's hut and waved a lantern with a light in it. Smashing, that was.'

He snorted. 'That's not difficult to do. I can make mine puff smoke if I want to. And look—I've got a tunnel with a contact just in front so the train hoots as it goes in. I'll show you.'

He turned a switch and set a transformer buzzing somewhere. A goods train in a siding full of coal gave a twitch. More lights came on and a signal arm fell outside a country station. A black LMS loco and tender with a snake of red coaches behind it chuntered along the track to my left with a stately whirr and a realistic clicking of wheels on rails. As it headed into a tree-covered hill in which a stone-edged tunnel mouth was set it gave a realistic wail and plunged out of sight.

'What about that?' demanded Charlie.

'Great. Whistler in the dark.'

'Eh?'

His eyes widened blankly at me above the thick black beard, dense and crinkly like a springy wire-wool brush.

'Whistler in the dark,' I said. 'The train in the tunnel. You used to see notices by the track that said "Whistle" before a tunnel or crossing. When I was at school we all used to whistle when we saw one and fall about. Schoolboy humour.'

'Oh. You still do. See them, I mean. I've got two or three dotted about here somewhere. They were wood, painted black, with big wood letters painted white. There's one, there.'

Beside a road crossing, to the left of the track, was a board with the single word 'Whistle' painted on it. I hadn't seen one for a long time. 'That's it,' I said. 'We thought they were funny.'

He gave a grin. 'You was easily pleased. What can I do you for, Tim? Looking for a Botticelli, are you?'

'Not exactly. You're a railway expert, Charlie. Does the name Winans mean anything to you?'

He switched off the transformer and the buzzing stopped. 'Course it does. Baltimore and Ohio. That's like the Stockton and Darlington is to us. First railway the Yanks ever 'ad. Winans—Ross Winans, that is, the father—he built the locos and the rolling stock, sometimes. His son was pretty hot too—Thomas, his name was—he was on that Russian line. Moscow—St Petersburg. He and his dad invented the four-wheel bogey at each end of a carriage. Everyone used it ever

84

since.'

'What else?'

His brow furrowed in concentration. 'What else? I don't know what else. There was one or two more of them but Ross and Thomas was the important ones.' He cocked his head on one side. 'There was another—can't remember his name—lived here in England, I'm not sure when. First World War time, I think. He had an estate with footmen in Russian livery and carriages. They made a lot of money in Russia, the Winans. Effing Yanks.' He flashed me a hard glance. 'I'll tell you something, Tim; they're a greedy bunch, Yanks are.'

'Oh, really? Having trouble with them, are you?'

He came across from his bench and stood facing me over the nearly six feet of track, stations and rolling woodland. His black face creased, into anger as he pointed past me to the door.

'Through there,' he said lividly, 'there's three fucking oak coffers I got for a Yank because he always buys them. He bought last year—four hundred quid each. That was six hundred dollars then. Didn't ask any questions, he didn't. Bought all I had. He comes in here last week and sees those three. "How much?" he says. "Four hundred cach," I says, "same as last year." "Too expensive," he says. "Too expensive?" I says. "Fucking hell, the pound's collapsed since last year and I'm asking no more for 'em. That's only four hundred dollars now." "Still too expensive," he says, "I want a lower price." You know what, Tim?' His face congested with anger.

'What?'

'It's the old story. They think we're finished so they can kick us when we're down. Treat us with contempt. Beat us down further; kick a man when he's on his knees. I says to him, "That's it," I says. "Out you go." "Hey," he says, "can't we talk about this?" "Talk about it," I says, "if you're not out that fucking door in five

85

seconds I'm going to throw you through it while it's shut," I says.'

He moved his menacing bulk closer to the table as the story gripped him. '"You can fuck off, Yank," I says, "and don't fucking well come back here or you'll be bloody sorry." He scarpered out the door like a shot rabbit, he did. I've still got those three coffers but I'm buggered if I'm selling them to some greasy Yank at below price; they can afford it but they just want to rub our noses in the dirt.'

'It was very silly of him,' I said, soothingly, 'but I'm afraid that is human nature. You always get kicked when you're down.'

'Not me, I don't. I don't need any bloody Yank to live off.'

He glowered at me for a moment. A look came into his eyes as though, now that it was off his chest, the resentment made him feel slightly guilty. His brow unscrewed its angry scowl and he turned slightly sideways, half-watching me.

'I heard a little story about you the other day,' he said, in a mild half-mocking tone.

'Little bird told me.'

'Did you now?'

'Yeah. I heard you was involved with poor old Harwell. Poor old sod.'

'You're still in touch with everything that happens in Chelsea, then, are you, Charlie?'

'Sure. I have to keep in with the Old Bill, don't I?' He grinned.

'Might lose me licence, like, if I don't.'

'Yes. It was dreadful.'

He nodded. 'Shocking. Old Freddie Harwell, now, the dad, he was a real good dealer, he was. Before my time but people still used to talk about him round here. He really knew his stuff, he did. The children—well, they're old now—the sister and his brother, the sickly one, they wasn't up to the old man's standard. It's often the way.

86

They retired a few years back. Comes to something, doesn't it? You work your life, your time comes to sit back with a bit of a nest egg and some rotten stinking sod comes along and smashes you up. It makes me sick, it does. There was a time, here in Chelsea, they wouldn't have dared do that. We'd have got them, for sure. But it's all outsiders now. You never know who anyone is.'

'It was horrible,' I said. 'Poor old man. And his sister— dead of shock really.'

'Yeah.'

'They're looking for the brother. Seaside somewhere.'

'Yeah, so I believe. He was never well, that one.'

'No?'

'Nah. Chesty, he was. Quiet as a mouse. Do they know where he is?'

I shrugged. 'I don't know. I suppose they'll find him.' A thought occurred to me. 'Do you know something? Whoever it was smashed up a lot of that Staffordshire the Harwells had, broke the Vicky pieces but not the rest. I reckon there was some early stuff that's disappeared.'

He gave an angry snort-grunt again. 'Well, that's not surprising, is it? Early Staffordshire's always been pricey. The Yanks have collected it for years. Popular over there, it is. They've been buying up the best bits for Christ knows how long. Fucking Yanks; they're greedy, Tim, they've got the money and they just take everything.'

'Now let's not start that again, Charlie. There might be no business at all without them.'

'It's not real business, Tim. Not for good old-fashioned long-established dealers. It's these new, hot-shot money boys that've buggered up the trade.' He moved back away from the layout and picked up the tiny screwdriver again.

'I'll stick to me trains, I will. And a fair turn now and again.'

'Take it easy, Charlie. You've a long time to go yet and

I've no doubt there's lots of deals in you still. Thanks for the info anyway. And if you can find anything more about the Winans I'd be very grateful. Particularly that one who had the estate in England.'

He nodded vaguely from his bench. 'Any time, Tim. I'll do me best. Give you a bell if it comes up.'

'OK. Cheers, Charlie.'

'Cheers, mate.'

I rattled my way out through the copper pans and stood out on the pavement, watching the dust and grit get blown by the blast of passing traffic. As I've said, there's not much left of Whistler's Chelsea.

CHAPTER 12

Nobby Roberts picked up his pint of bitter, downed the remaining two or three inches of it, put it down and glared suspiciously at the ploughman's lunch on the plate on the table in front of him.

'Look at that butter,' he said, disgustedly. 'In little metallized paper packets. It's disgraceful. Why can't they give you a proper piece of butter from a slab, like they used to?'

'Progress,' I responded cheerfully. 'Hygiene. Less value for money. They all go together.'

His sandy-red hair fell over one eye. 'What bloody ploughman ever carried butter in little metal-paper packets? Eh? I ask you that.'

'Now come on, Nobby, you know very well, because you've seen the film, that a Ploughman's Lunch never really existed. Some ad men invented it in the 'sixties as a way of getting people into pubs. It's doubtful if a real ploughman carried bread, butter, cheese and pickle with him. He used to have a pound of cold bacon, a peck of beans and a quart of ale. The ale was sweet sticky stuff that would have given all of us a dose of the screaming habdabs.'

'Apart from laying us out cold,' seconded Charles Massenaux.

'True. Absolutely true. Modern beer is thin washy stuff that ploughmen would have called small beer. They drank it instead of water. I'd better get us all another one.'

'Just a half for me,' said Charles hastily.

'Rubbish. Never trust a man who drinks halves. It's a pint or nothing.'

We were in the Doctor Watson. It's a pub off Whitehall, in neutral ground, to which Charles had sauntered from his auction rooms and Nobby had strode from New Scotland Yard. I felt a bit guilty about the name of the pub; Nobby is terribly sensitive about jokes about detectives, the police, that sort of thing. Today, however, he was too preoccupied to notice. The pub was full; it was a lunch-time place mainly and I could imagine that it would be a bit sombre at night. Now, however, it was noisy and raucous, with junior civil servants of definitely non-Oxbridge origins clashing their glasses at the bar. One tried to push past me and then thought better of it; I must have glared at him.

'So,' I said, when I had got back to our table, 'what's the news, Nobby? Come on, we're all agog.'

I guessed he was reluctant. I mean, if you or your team have solved the case, found the missing man, clicked the 'cuffs on the criminal and restored order, you're not slow to tell everyone. Nobby hadn't said a word; not a single dicky-bird. He glowered at his beer. Then he gave a sort of rueful laugh and smiled at us.

'We can't find the brother,' he admitted, 'let alone get a lead on your pair, Tim.'

Sue and I had done it all down at the station. Identikit pictures made up, scanned the local Rogues Gallery—a set of volumes of photographs of the local hard boys and, it seemed, most of London's criminal fraternity— the lot. We'd been there for hours. I gaped at him.

'But surely,' I said 'you must have found the brother's address at the house? They must have written to him, kept letters, an address book, surely?'

He shook his head. 'Everything about him has been carefully omitted. It's as though they deliberately kept him secret. There is no record of any kind of his address in that house. Johnson is getting bloody frustrated, I can tell you. And the one lead he has got, which they've followed up locally, hasn't come to anything yet. It means it's going to take time. That always helps the other side.' He glanced at Charles. 'Tim has described the paintings in the photographs to you? The missing photos of the paintings, I mean?'

Charles nodded. 'Yes, he has. Very interesting.'

'What do you think?'

90

He shrugged. 'Impossible to tell until I see the actual paintings. They might be genuine. Whistler hasn't been very widely faked, although there have been some attempts. Even at the etchings, too; they fetch a few thousand each if they're the right ones. A lot of his work disappeared during his lifetime. That school he set up in Paris at the very end of his life—the one Gwen John went to—he was in partnership with a model of his, a woman he painted from childhood to maturity. She was called Carmen Rossi. A powerful lady; it was supposed to be called the Academic Whistler but everyone called it the Academic Carmen. When the school was folding up due to Whistler's age and illness, she pinched quantities of his work from his studio. Freer bought several from her after Whistler's death; he must have guessed that they were stolen.'

'Surely,' I interposed, 'the Harwell pictures are from a much earlier period? I mean, Wapping was painted around 1860 so this one must be from around then? And Maud Franklin belongs to the early 1870s and 1880s; she was gone around 1887 when Whistler married Godwin's widow, Trixie.'

'Of course. Whistler was declared bankrupt in 1879, after the famous trial against Ruskin. His house and studio were sold up. The contents fetched very little; Thomas Way bought a vast hoard of unfinished canvases for a guinea. Howell got charge of the Mother portrait which Graves owned against a debt. So it's possible these two could have got away then, but most of his important work is well documented.'

'Nevertheless, Whistler was a secretive man in many ways. He could have kept them to one side?'

'Oh, very easily. Or Howell might have. Or a spare mistress. We'd have to see them.'

Nobby grunted. 'Bugger the bloody paintings, then. What we want is to find the killers.'

I thought of Sue, her face white, her conviction about the two men. 'The paintings are the key, Nobby.

Wherever they are and whatever they are, the intruders were after them. They took the photographs.'

He nodded reluctantly. 'Johnson says the same thing. That's why he's so keen to find the brother. Leonard, his name is, apparently.'

'What's the lead you've got? The one you mentioned?'

There was silence. He took a swallow of his beer.

'Nobby?'

Charles Massenaux gave me a curious glance. He cocked his eyebrows up in a query, glancing quickly towards Nobby and back to me again in silent perplexity.

'Nobby?'

He sighed. 'Look here, Tim, this is a police matter. We have a lead and we're following it up. We don't need any amateur assistance.'

'Charming.'

He flushed. 'You know what you're like. If I give you the slightest fraction of an inch you'll take five miles. The less you know the better.'

Charles grinned sardonically. 'Back in your hole, Tim. No finding the missing Leonard, wherever he is—where was it, you said?'

I glared at them both. 'The seaside, somewhere.'

'Oh well, that's easy!' Charles chuckled provocatively. 'Very easy! Anyone with the name Leonard would quite naturally head for the most obvious resort!' He leered at me with a knowing smile.

My jaw dropped. I nearly knocked my beer over as I stabbed a finger at him. 'Of course! Good grief! His patron saint! Nobby? Are we right? It can't be, can it?'

Nobby had gone bright red. His sandy hair fell across his pink-tinged eyes. Charles slapped his thigh in joy.

'St Leonards! It has to be!'

'Look at Nobby! It is!'

For a moment I thought he was going to burst into fury but he suddenly laughed. 'I don't know why I speak to you two! I'm admitting nothing.'

'How very appropriate.' Charles was enjoying himself. 'Don't you agree, Tim?'

'Appropriate?' My mind whirred. What did he mean?

'Come on; you with your devious mind full of biographical details. What connects St Leonards with Whistler?'

I frowned. Nobby's face was blank.

'Think. A clue for you, then; what do you connect St Leonards with?'

'Well, the coast, of course, and Hastings, and—' I stopped. Charles grinned broadly. 'Christ! I've got it!'

Nobby scowled. 'When you two have quite finished: is this likely to be of use to me? Because if so—' He left the sentence unfinished but he leant across the table in alert attention.

'Shall I tell him or will you?'

Charles gave me a mock bow. 'You do it, Tim. He's your old chum, after all.'

I bowed in response and took a swig of bitter before speaking. 'Hastings and St Leonards are almost indistinguishable. There are three parallel valleys, side by side, leading to the sea. One has the old town of Hastings in it, the middle one is Hastings proper and the third is St Leonards. They're packed together.'

'So?'

'So you've heard of Whistler's mother? Anna McNeill Whistler? The one in the portrait, now in the Louvre? Miserable-looking old church-goer.'

'Of course I have. Come to the point, for Christ's sake.'

'She's buried in Hastings. She lived there for the last five years of her life.'

He put down his glass. He looked at us both in turn. 'I don't like this,' he said.

'It's probably pure coincidence.'

'But it's bloody close. Did she have any paintings?'

We both shrugged. 'I doubt it,' Charles said, 'unless it was the odd sketch. Whistler was too hard up to give

93

much to his mother, even though she kept house for him in Chelsea for a while.'

'She was a religious freak,' I said. 'Got in the way of his amorous frolics. I think he was quite relieved when she had to go to Hastings for her health.'

'Still,' said Charles, ever humorous, 'it won't be hard to find Leonard Harwell in a place like St Leonard's, surely?'

Nobby looked moody. 'There's no one by the name of Harwell in St Leonard's. Not in the phone book, not anywhere. We got the lead from a Cadogan Walk neighbour, an old woman who remembered the time when he left Chelsea. He chose St Leonard's because of his own name; she knew that. You'd be surprised how hard it is to find missing people. It's bloody difficult. The local force are trying but, as I said, it'll take time. That gives the other side a chance.'

He finished his beer and shot me a look. 'I don't like to remind you, Tim, but Hastings has unfortunate connotations for you and me. I wouldn't like them repeated. We've put out local messages in and on the media for Harwell to contact us. So don't get any ideas, will you?'

'Of course not. Supposing he doesn't though? Contact you, I mean.'

'Leave it to us.'

'Yes, Nobby.'

Charles gave me a sardonic look. 'I must be going. Pretend to use this Friday afternoon, what's left of it, constructively. Thanks for the lunch, Tim. See you both around, as they say.'

'I'd almost forgotten. Saturday tomorrow, thank God.'

How useful, I thought as Nobby left, too; Sue could do with a nice drive out of town. They say that sea air is good for you, sometimes. Just the thing after a business dinner with a prospective American client.

CHAPTER 13

Jeremy White bought his London house twenty years ago, when people thought that thirty-odd thousand pounds was a fortune to pay for a property. Jeremy was in his mid-twenties and was already showing the sense of investment flair that he was to exploit much later. The Bank had him stuck in a lowly position and frowned upon his activities but Jeremy, as ever, blandly ignored the Bank. Even when he was sent away to the Far East to do his ritual term of service in the family's far-flung empire he retained possession of the house, which was divided into three flats then. Jeremy kept the top one for himself and allowed the rents from the other two to pay the interest on the mortgage loan he had acquired. The house was run-down and seedy; the square to which it belonged, between Knightsbridge and South Kensington, was a half-backwater bounded by a small crescent on one side which gave it an odd, irregular shape of great charm, enhanced by the thick trees in the centre.

He occupied the whole house now, having spread himself downwards from top to bottom as each flat occupant departed. Like most of the houses in the square it had been thoroughly renovated structurally, re-plumbed and rewired. The ground floor, above the cellars, had a sort of reception-dining-room set in front of the kitchen, which extended backwards via a handsome conservatory into the small back garden. After a very civilized dinner in this area we had withdrawn upstairs to the sitting-room proper, which was on the first floor, at the front of the house, with long French windows overlooking the square. It was a fine London room in what had once been considered a modest house for the middle class, now affordable only by the wealthy. The proportion was square, with a good moulded ceiling painted white while the walls, below the cornice, were a warm buttermilk fabric with a fine vertical line. The carpet and curtains were a deeper hue, not quite caramel, but this evenness of tone was broken by splashes of colour from the chairs and sofa coverings, a splendid Kazak rug and a great dazzling blue chinoiserie long-case clock with pagoda top and brass finials capping a magnificent silver-brass-faced month movement by Knibb.

There was an eighteenth-century seascape by Brooking, always a rich man's painter, and a frigate off the Cape by Thomas Whitcomb. These and a nineteenth-century painting of a yacht race off Cowes were reflections of Jeremy's interest in sailing and I knew he had bought them years ago for what was now little money. The advent of Mary had brought two fine flower paintings to the room, one by Linnel, and a pair of terriers by Landseer. A gilt Chippendale mirror hung on the pier wall between the French windows, over a crisp mahogany card table shaped for candlestands and scoops. The fireplace under the Brooking was ample, functional, fendered in brass. It was obviously a room reserved for occasions, but still warm; the sofa and chairs were comfortable. Casey lounged in one of them by the window while I, with him, looked out over the lighted square. Mary and Sue had excused themselves to withdraw upstairs to talk about babies, in which Sue was showing an alarming interest and knowledge. Jeremy had gone genially down to the cellars to trace an exceptional bottle of port. We were now on first-name terms with Casey, who turned out, not surprisingly, to be an Andy.

'This is delightful,' he said. 'I must say that Mary seems to know a fantastic amount about our kind of banking.'

'She used to be secretary to Jeremy's uncle, Sir Richard White. He was Chairman of the Bank until a few months ago.'

'Oh, I see. So Jeremy married her while she was at the Bank?'

'Er, not exactly. Shortly after Sir Richard left. There was what you might call something of a coup d'etat. She stayed on for a month or two after they married but they decided to start a family fairly briskly so she's somewhat hors de combat now.'

He smiled. 'And your lady, Sue. She's your, um, er, she's your—'

'Something like that,' I smiled back at him. 'Sue and I have been together for a while now. But we're not married.'

'I see. She really knows a hell of a lot about art. When you and Mary were talking I asked about one or two things that interest me and she really did know it all backwards. Wow. She should write a book on the French Impressionists.'

'I'm afraid rather a lot of other people have already done that. I didn't know you were keen on art.'

'Well, I'm nothing like in your people's category but I have a Remington and we do buy paintings for the Bank. You know, modern things mainly, contemporary Americans. But as I told you, I'd heard of your Art Fund. I admire that. You seem to have done well with it.'

'It's gone quite satisfactorily, yes.'

'Has your, er, Sue, does she get involved? As an adviser, I mean?'

'She has done on occasion.' I didn't like to tell him on what occasions; they always seemed to turn violent.

'I think your English girls are fantastic. They have such charm, really they do. And those two are a fantastic combination.'

'That's a compliment, coming from a man who's just arrived from Brazil.'

He grinned. 'I think I should remind you that I'm a married man with three children. And we are Catholics from way back.'

'So are most of the Brazilians.'

He laughed then, crinkling his freckled face into an unabashed grimace of pleasure so that it was difficult for me, in a way, to say to him, 'Tell me, what on earth did you come to see us for?'

He stopped laughing. His face set. 'Hey, you don't pull any punches, do you?'

'Sorry. That was a bit abrupt, but it was Brazil that brought it about. I can't see why you came to see us. If you wanted to set up a counter-trade deal with White's—and why not with another American bank is another question too—then surely the logical thing would have been to do it with White's Brazil? You didn't need the London end particularly.'

'Well, let's just say I like to deal with the centre of things.'

'Oh. But in this case the banks are autonomous. It's like, say, choosing to deal with Lazard Frères in New York or in Paris. Or Lazard Brothers in London. The most appropriate one is usually in the country concerned.'

'Sure, I understand that. But I was coming to London anyway and you did set up the manufacturer's deal here even though the main negotiators were in Brazil. I was very impressed with White's in Brazil. Damn it, your James not only knew Figueredo, he was an old friend of Tancredo Neves. It's a damned shame Tancredo died.'

'Oh yes. Tancredo came from Minas Gerais which is where James worked for many years. He's practically a Mineiro, like Tancredo was.'

'With contacts like that he must be in a pretty impressive position. I mean, he'll have other similar ones?'

'James is going great guns in Brazil.'

'Right.' He hesitated and I decided to let him say what he wanted without pressure. A lower lip curled up over his upper one in a grimace of decision. 'To be honest, James wasn't very complimentary about your London operation.'

'That sounds like James all right.'

'He wasn't actually disloyal or anything. In the States we would disapprove very strongly of that. What he said was that if I was going to visit with White's London office I should make sure that I only spoke with Jeremy White and you. I won't tell you what he said about the others. These two are the ones for you to see, he said. "Jeremy and a henchman of his called Simpson" were his exact words.'

'Henchman. Gruff old buzzard, he is.'

Casey smiled again. 'I don't think he was so far from the reality of things.'

I gave a half-grunt. Jeremy came carefully into the room carrying a decanter. 'I'm most frightfully sorry about this,' he murmured, 'really I am. Frightfully slack. Should have been decanted hours ago. But I rather thought you might like this; it's often very acceptable.'

He poured out three glasses and brought them, carefully across to us, giving Casey his first. It was a great port and the American's eyebrows went high in appreciation. 'Superb,' he said, with awe in his voice.

'We've just been broaching the subject of Brazil,' I explained to Jeremy 'and why Andy needed to see us in London.'

'Oh dear! Andy, I do hope that Tim hasn't been putting you through it? He's an ex-rugger player, you know, scrum forward or something, can't help charging at things like a bull at a gate. It really is too bad of you, Tim, before we've had our port.'

'Not at all.' Casey's tolerant humour seemed genuine. 'I used to be a football player myself. Different rules but same principle once the whistle goes.'

'Well, really. That's very good of you. I suppose what has bothered Tim and me just a tiny bit—merely a sort of afterthought, really—is why you've come to us and not one of your own countrymen in this field?'

'That's a fair question.' Casey was not the slightest perturbed. 'I think you fellows are far too modest, though. You have a real facility for financing reciprocal-trade deals with Brazil and you obviously have the means for disposing of the counter-purchase goods involved here in England and in Europe. That's a very useful capacity to have. Now, OK, I appreciate that you will say to yourselves why does this fellow, this Yankee, come to see us when he can go to an American bank and they'll set up a similar deal? I'll tell you.'

He took another sip of his port, swallowed, looked pleased and sipped again. Jeremy carefully refilled his glass.

'Let me put it this way. Owens, McLeod and Casey is a bit like White's in reverse. We are essentially a domestic investment bank in the USA. Until recently we've never needed to be anything else. Hell, there's been more than enough business for us and our clients to keep us all busy and satisfied. If you're an anvil manufacturer in Topeka, Kansas, you could sell enough anvils in the Mid-West to keep you happy and in funds, never mind in California. As for abroad, well, that's best left alone. We've got clients in Illinois who've never heard of a Letter of Credit payable on shipment, let alone seen one. If you gave them one, they'd probably light their cigar with it. So it's just not been an area where we needed to operate.'

'Not at all?'

'Nope. Well, hardly. Canada, of course. Mexico occasionally. But not much: not a significant part of business. We opened up offices on the East and West coast, sure, and down in Texas. But not particularly for foreign trade. Now what happens? Our clients in Chicago and Cleveland and Albany and Baltimore decide they need to export, to take opportunities abroad. What happens? If we set up deals with some of the big New York boys we're into the jungle. They'll honour the first deal, sure, but what happens after that? Our clients know—then—that we have to use the services of one of the big boys. They'll start saying to themselves now how much extra was it for Owens, McLeod & Casey to cut in?

Those big banks are supermarkets: they offer everything, you name it. Export finance, counter-trade, corporate finance, equity issues, mergers and acquisitions, stock swaps, introductions, takeovers, hell they're not exactly *shy*, you know. They're beating round the doors the whole time like the clearing banks are. We need to give our clients the service ourselves as much as possible.'

'And White's would fit in without disturbing your clients' balance?'

'That's it.'

There was a silence. I finished my port and Jeremy refilled my glass. 'Well,' he said 'that seems very logical, I must say, don't you, Tim?'

'Yes. Yes, it does.' I tried to make my voice sound enthusiastic.

'Of course we're only too willing to market our, er, expertise in this field. So if we can get our heads together and put some numbers to things I'm sure it would be the next step, don't you?'

'Fine.' Casey's voice was hopeful. 'I'd like to do that. I'm going to get some details together, then I'll come and see you. How about Monday afternoon?'

'OK. Fine. Let's say two o'clock on Monday. Ah, here come the ladies.' Jeremy rose in stately welcome to Mary and Sue.

'We're invading you,' said Mary cheerfully. 'It's too fine a night to miss sitting here and looking out over the trees. Don't you agree, Andy? Aren't they beautiful?'

'Indeed so,' he replied gallantly. 'And to miss such pleasant company would be a shame. Actually we have this image of London always being foggy in the fall but I've not seen a pea-souper yet.'

'We don't really get pea-soupers any more. Not since they stopped burning coal. But we do get an occasional fog. It's funny how these images persist; it's like us always thinking that Chicago is full of gangsters.'

He laughed. 'Well, we do still have a few of those. They just don't carry tommy-guns and wear fedoras any more.'

'How unsporting,' Jeremy said. 'It must be hard to tell them from ordinary people.'

'You bet.' A glint came into Casey's eye. 'Some of them probably look like investment bankers.'

We all laughed at that and the conversation moved away into more topical subjects. Eventually we put Casey into a taxi back to his hotel and Sue and I took another over to Onslow Gardens.

'He's nice,' Sue said, when we got in. 'Very nice. There's something very masculine about that sort of American. And lots of charm.'

'That's the Irish. Always comes out.'

'Tall, too. And so *lean*. Very attractive.'

'Now, listen. Remember my South American upbringing.'

'What does that mean?'

'You playa around, I slitta your throat. Comprende?'

'How very primitive,' she said. 'Not like an investment banker at all.'

Then she kissed me with a ferocity I hadn't roused for a long time.

CHAPTER 14

St Mary's Terrace perches in a thin wavering line on the steep hillslope overlooking the central Hastings valley leading to the sea. Cars park out on high ledges with a metal balcony-rail around them in front of the house where Anna McNeill Whistler died. No. 43 is a narrow white house with bow windows set single-width, one on top of the other, in a trim threesome. Once it was called Talbot House, though the resounding name belies the small bright dwelling wedged into the row which supports it. I cocked an eye along the wandering lane, guessing house dates: Regency, early nineteenth century, perhaps a few late eighteenth. Then I turned back to the balcony-rail, leant on it, gazed at the choked sprawl of Hastings below me and lifted my eyes up to the slaggy scree of the railway line the other side.

Away to my left the sea glinted in the sun; just below me backyards of big red-brick terraces that Anna Whistler would never have seen, presented cold square wells of gritty neglect. Within a few degrees elevation a panorama of broad valley sweep, town and sea shone bright with cheerful potential. It was difficult to believe that if I had walked up the hill to my left, over the top of the grass headland above the castle, where Jimmy Whistler once strode in remorse with his brother Willie after their mother's death, I could have looked on two wildly contrasting views.

To the east the medieval Old Town, clogged in another, steeper valley full of picturesque timbered buildings that are sealed off from the seafront by fun-fairs, chip-shops and penny arcades. To the west, the far ocean-liner architecture and concrete decking of Marine Court, St Leonards, beached beside the Channel in nineteen-thirties redundancy on the distant promenade. Between the two lies the incredible tangle of modern Hastings and St Leonards: an urban pile of Regency, Victorian and modern buildings jumbled together in a variegated architectural bran-tub of prize exhibits and disqualified non-starters. It was a prospect to make you think, especially on a Saturday morning after a long and frustrating drive down from London.

If you were in the mood, I thought, you could draw some uncomfortable parallels with Hastings. In the 1870s and 1880s it was prosperous, confident and secure. The new centre to the west of the old medieval town was expanding. It had four theatres, a new station and a booming holiday trade. To Anna McNeill Whistler it must have seemed full of life. Big terraces of commodious houses went up, row by row, broad square by broad square, tall and commanding, with many bedrooms for big families or for letting to those who came to stay, who 'took lodgings' at the seaside, not only for just two weeks. Great mansions went up on the ridge above the town. The promenade was developed, a central clock tower put up. The middle valley was made into public gardens for recreation with a bandstand. The very centre, close to the sea, sported a fine cricket ground. Drains were dug. Building went on at every level, in the valley and even up the steep hill-slopes, near to the castle, above it. Fishing thrived, celebrities came to stay. An imposing pier was run out into the sea to rival that of Eastbourne and those of Brighton. There were grand hotels, a bracing beach, fine views, big churches, classical chapels and meeting-rooms. There was much need for furnishings, clothing, food, drink, domestic services, transport and pubs with cheerful barmaids. There was much poverty.

The First World War was a blow that numbed the nerves of everyone. Fortunately, despite the impact, life went on. The 'twenties and 'thirties saw the outside of the town expand in modern ribbon-development, with neat rows of desirable semi-detached houses stringing the edges of every road. Industry, protected from imports, provided jobs for the semi-dwellers, financed their mortgages, pensioned some of the retired. The town responded gallantly to the Hitler War. It was in the front line; the people behaved with tremendous courage. After that, nothing went right.

In modern Hastings the visitor can stand awed at the once-grand buildings, the solid classical embellishment constructed by people who built for ever, now eaten by the harsh sea air and divided for a lesser set of purposes. Some have fallen down. It is a town of great 'character', as an old actor in a nursing home might be so described, with erudite fusty bookshops jostling rows of fish cafés. Everything caters for the cheapest denominator. The clock tower has gone to allow for a central one-way traffic system that neither helps pedestrians nor speeds traffic. The churches and hotels struggle for a sinking survival. The town has the highest unemployment in the South-East. Its communications are derelict: the railway neglected, the only road to London a country lane. New factory estates try to soak up some of the workers lying idle; they are not enough. The fishing-boats are obsolete; foreigners catch the fish. The town council squabbles over how and whether the central cricket ground should be built on or not; London prevaricates. There is no coherent development plan, no driving policy; there are preservation groups clinging to the past, who obstruct. The people seem powerless to effect any change. They are becoming nervous, resentful, insecure and quarrelsome. Their friends and neighbours from outside, fond of the town, seeing its potential, its great character, liking its people and admiring their intelligence, shake their heads sadly and depart, wondering if it will contrive to sink into the sea. It is in a strange, timeless triangle of land, missing the pulse and booming development that passes by on either side of it. No one is actually starving but the easiest thing to do would be to blow it up, demolish it and start all over again.

I shook myself. Morbid thoughts prey in places that have bad memories. Nobby had a point about me and him and Hastings. There was poor Belgie Klooster, murdered in his shop on the seafront, when I had first met Marianne Gray, busy faking Godwin sideboards. It was only a year or so ago; too close, too near, too disquieting.

Sue was watching me curiously. Her brown hair blew in the breeze and her blue eyes, narrowed into the sunlight, focused keenly on me.

'You were miles away,' she stated. 'What were you thinking of? Or, dare I ask, who were you thinking of?'

With a woman's perception, she knew; my previous experiences in Hastings, incurred while Sue was away in Australia, were all part of our past history and she knew most of the salient facts. I wondered if she guessed, too, that I had made love to Marianne Gray in that same car, the Volvo, on the old sea cliffs above Wittersham, diverted from Hastings by a careful appeal to my baser appetites. I put my arm around her.

'Not what or who you're thinking of,' I said. 'Just having a brood on the nature of things generally. How this area is a microcosm of a wider malaise. And thinking of what Whistler's mother must have seen from this point. She was looked after by a couple who ran the house for five years. It must have been much more open then; not nearly so built up.

She gave me a quiet look, face close, that showed only half a belief in my answer. The texture of her clothes was warm and soft, faintly scented. There was something about Sue that I knew I never wanted to lose, never wanted to leave behind. Perhaps that was why I'd taken it so badly when she went to Australia, when she left me. I squeezed her tightly.

'Ow!' she protested. 'You're crushing me!'

'Sorry.' I released her and noticed the occasional curious face in the windows of the jumbled terrace, the stares at unknown visitors in their narrow unvisited spot. You have to be determined to find St Mary's Terrace, or to live in it, to be there.

'What are you going to do now?'

Eh?'

'Now that we're here and you've found the house that Anna Whistler lived and died in, where do you go to next? How are you going to find old Leonard Harwell?'

'Oh, that's easy.'

'Is it? How?'

'We'll go to St Leonards,' I said, leading her back to the Volvo. 'A man like that could never stay very far from the trade, that's for sure. It'll be a cinch.'

I rolled her over the headland, down past the castle ruins and dog-legged on to the promenade, turning west. The light was dazzling and she gave a cry of pleasure, briefly, at the prancing sea and the pier. As we approached St Leonards, however, before we got to Warrior Square, she turned to me.

'Where was it?' she demanded.

I stopped. To our right a row of shops broke the stolid boarding-house terrace of the seafront.

'There,' I said, pointing.

It was a fish restaurant. You would never have guessed, if you hadn't known, that Belgie Klooster and his boys used to fill that space with furniture, most of it junk, en route to the Continent. There was no sign of its former use. It seemed to reassure Sue: she gave a little shiver but then she nodded as though something had cleared in her mind. An episode was over. 'Let's go,' she said.

I let in the clutch and passed the open space of a once-grand Warrior Square, where tubular scaffolding, angled in the gaps, now props up the big terrace houses facing the sea. At the turn to the high street leading up the hill I had to stop at the traffic lights and put down the sun visor to shade my eyes from the light, as they had done in the big Ford Granada that pulled up behind me. Almost as soon as I turned right, up the hill, I turned left into Norman Road, allowing the Granada to go on past my tail as I took the corner. Norman Road runs parallel with the sea but one block in and up, above the promenade line, and is not very wide, so it seems much darker when you turn out of the sea-light. The houses are rather like Anna Whistler's but there is a gothic Methodist church and 'thirties cinema, now used for other purposes. There is also a clutch of antique shops; it's the centre of the St Leonards trade.

I put the Volvo into a parking space by the pavement, grunting as I got out against the slope. Sue swung out easily on her side and we took a turn up and down the street; stripped pine, 'thirties furniture, general rubbish, Victoriana, trade only. It was a fair cross-section but the type of shop I wanted was halfway up.

'In here,' I indicated to Sue and plunged in with a jangle of bells.

It was a woman's shop. You can always tell. The few bits of furniture were small. There were a lot of ornaments and decorative things, brackets and needlework. Miniatures, watercolours and prints. Best of all, though, were the shelves and the big glass display-case I'd seen through the window.

A lot of the china was bright trash; the display-case was nearly full of Doulton, all grey and blue and brown, rather subfusc and solid, with serious urns next to high-minded vases. But there was some Staffordshire, cheerfully vulgar and smeary, on two shelves in the display-case, sitting close to the Doulton rather like a fairground set up next to a hospital. I couldn't help smiling at it.

The shop had an office-room in the back corner, with a curtain across the door and a half-silvered mirror-window so that the occupant could see the interior. As I stepped across the floor the curtain moved and a woman came out, giving me an open, appraising stare before she glanced quickly at Sue behind me. I put her as slightly older than me, late thirties perhaps, and therefore about ten years older than Sue. She was fair-haired, probably dyed, and open-faced, almost bold but without the hard defensive look that women dealers get. Behind her, through the curtained gap I could see a chaise-longue jammed against the office wall, a roll-top bureau full of papers, and a chair. She gave me an open smile.

'Hello,' she said. 'Looking for something particular?'
Her gaze flicked up and down me again and I sensed a slight stiffness congealing Sue. I grinned back at her.

'Looking for help,' I said. 'But it's an old man I'm after, I'm afraid.'

Her head tilted back and her grin broadened. 'Now why would I have any *old* men?' she demanded. 'Do I look the type?'

I laughed. 'No—I'm sorry. I'll explain.' Briefly I tried to describe what I imagined old Harwell would look like, using his dead brother as a model for size, appearance and character. I didn't go into all the reasons why he was being looked for: I hinted that it was much to his advantage and that he'd been lost trace of since his brother had 'died'.

She shook her head. 'Sorry. Don't know anyone like that.'

'Staffordshire,' I urged. 'He must buy Staffordshire. I don't think he can drive so he must potter around here sometimes. An old man. He'll buy all kinds of Stafford-shire, good and bad. He's probably crazy about it but he was in the trade, in London, so he'll buy cagily.'

'Oh. You must mean Mr Howell. At least that's how he pronounces it. Not Harwell. Howell.' She glanced to me and then Sue and back again. 'Is anything the matter? He's a little man, not like you say, smaller. In his seventies, I'd say. Just like a mouse. Lives up the hill somewhere. He buys Staffordshire. Always asks for trade discount. Had a business in the King's Road years ago.'

Sue and I stared at each other. Prickles ran down the back of my neck. 'Howell? Are you sure?'

The woman turned her hands up. 'That's the only one who comes anywhere close. Don't see him often; maybe once a month. Must be that long since he was last in.'

'Where does he live?'

She shook her head. 'Sorry. Don't know. He pays cash. Up the hill there somewhere; you know what it's like— all bedsitters and flats. They come and go. Never known anything like this place; I've only been here two years, I was in Portsmouth before and I thought ships that pass in the night, I thought, I'll go somewhere stable, you know, but St Leonards is no different.' She gave me another appraising stare. 'You're in the trade too, are you?'

'Sort of. Look here—could you think of anyone else who might know where Harwell—I mean Mr Howell— lives?'

Her brow furrowed. 'I could ask. Or he might come in. He always paid cash so I've no invoices.' She winked. 'Don't like invoices anyway. Have you asked the others?'

'No. I doubt if he'd visit them. Staffordshire's his thing.'

'In that case I'm his only port of call here.' She gave another sympathetic smile. 'Have you got a card? Leave your number; I'll ring you if I find anything. That's all I can do.'

I got out a card and wrote my home number on the back of it before handing it over. She gave a low whistle.

'White's! Well, well. We *are* moving in big circles now. Couldn't interest you in some nice Doulton, could I?' She gestured at her display-case.

'If you help me to find old Harwell, or Howell, I promise I'll buy your best piece. Please, please try for me?'

'OK.' She cocked her head on one side. 'I'll do that. Be glad to have you back again.'

Sue said nothing until we were back in the Volvo, buckling on our seat-belts. Her lips were compressed. She gave me a schoolmistressy look.

'It's a very good thing I came with you!'

'Why? What's up?'

'That hussy! She'd have had you into her office and on to her chaise-longue in two ticks! Portsmouth! I can imagine what she did there!'

'Sue, really! Women dealers are never like that. They're much too defensive with men.'

'Ha!'

I started the engine. 'You must admit that I found the right place.'

'Oh yes! Just like a homing pigeon!'

'I meant Harwell, you silly girl. It's astounding; why does he call himself Howell?'

'If it's him.'

'It must be. It fits so closely.' I drove carefully up the back streets. 'He has to be here somewhere.'

To the west of St Leonards high street there's a strange lost area of huge old terraces that make you feel, temporarily, as though you have strayed into one of London's rotting inner boroughs. They are classical or Italianate houses going up three, four or five storeys with attics above, encrusted on the façades with pediments and mouldings or those arcaded window archings that remind one of Osborne and Sir Charles Barry. Caught between Septimus Burton's grottoed valley and the main shop-fronted road to the sea there's almost a square mile of bedsitter and flat-land inhabited by God knows who supported by an unknown economy. Parts of it have been repainted and smartened up; multiple doorbells attest to internal refurbishment. Parts of it are stained, dirty and crumbling, splashed with permanent damp from broken down-pipes and guttering. I drove round the dismal streets in helpless frustration, racking my brains to work out the best system for flushing out old Leonard Harwell. I couldn't think of one; why did he call himself Howell?

At least, I thought, each time I go uphill I don't need the sun visor to block out the sun and obscure the view because it's behind me. I can put the visor up. Unlike the two men in the Ford Granada coming up the street. They had theirs down, making their faces invisible which was odd, considering.

It was the same Ford Granada. From the seafront traffic lights.

I turned left, then right, up a hill cuffed by lines of towering terraces, right again, and stopped at a junction, waiting.

'What are you doing?' Sue inquired, shifting uncomfortably. 'Are you hoping to see him in the street?'

The Granada came out of the turn I'd just made and eased its way towards me without any hurry. The visors were still down. The sun was nowhere near in their eyes.

I swung left down a short street lined with shabby cars and came to the main high street again, higher up, on the route to London. Turning left, I headed uphill following the signs out of town.

'We're wasting time,' I said to Sue shortly. 'There's nothing we can do here. I made a mistake: let's leave it to the police. I'll buy you lunch on the way home.'

The Granada came out of the same side-street and turned in our direction. I accelerated faster up the hill. Sue turned a surprised face to me. 'You're giving up? Just like that? But we were so close, you said.'

'Well, we tried.' I flicked a glance into the mirror. The Granada was closing. 'Maybe the dealer-woman will find this man calling himself Howell. I've got her card. I'll keep phoning her.' It had steadied now, about fifty yards back, but Sue caught my second flick of the eyes to the mirror. She swung right round in her seat, then she looked at me, concentrating on the road.

'There's something wrong! Tim? What is it?' Her voice went a tone higher.

'I think we're being followed.'

She stiffened. 'Who by? For heaven's sake!'

'A Ford Granada. Behind us.'

She swung round again and stared at it. I turned off the main London road at the junction outside St Leonards' leading to Battle, went about a mile up the road slowly and turned right into a housing estate. The Granada flashed by. I blew out a long breath and half-relaxed.

'Perhaps I was mistaken,' I said, spreading my fingers on the wheel.

Sue licked her lips. Her face gained colour again. 'You gave me a terrible fright. Who could they have been?'

I shook my head and began to pick the way through the estate back towards the main London road. 'That's the trouble with this sort of thing. You start to jump at shadows.' I patted her hand. 'Sorry, Sue. It's still not much use prowling round St Leonards, though. If the old boy is Leonard Harwell then the very fact that he's using a false name, however close to his own, is going to make finding him very difficult. I'll tell Nobby about it— no, I'd better not. If he gets to hear that I've been out doing a bit of amateur sleuthing he'll have an apoplectic fit. You know what he's like.'

Sue smiled. 'Dear Nobby. No, you'd better not.' She smoothed down her skirt. 'I'm hungry, Tim. Where are we having lunch?'

'Oh, I'll stop at a pub in Pembury or somewhere.'

'Well, come on, then. It's nearly one o'clock.' She glanced quickly back over her shoulder. 'There's no one behind. This investigative business has given me an appetite. That or the sea air.'

'Rubbish. It's that bran you eat at breakfast.'

She gave me a sharp prod and I grinned as I sped up the road, through Robertsbridge and Hurst Green, passing the Battle turn with a quick glance for the Granada. There was no sign of it. Nevertheless, I thought, as the car wound down the hill into Lamberhurst, they might have gone ahead and parked up a side-road somewhere, you never can tell. It would be silly to upset Sue again, though, so I decided not to tell her to keep an eye out; she'd had enough tension due to the Harwells already.

Going out of Lamberhurst there's a steep hill, with a fork right at the top for Horsmonden. I kept straight on the London—Tonbridge road and glanced quickly in the mirror to see back down the main street of the village; there was nothing in view. It gave me a false sense of security. As we reached the top of the hill I eased up on the left-hand bend, seeing a heavy lorry up ahead that was bound to slow us down; you can't overtake on that steep and winding stretch. It's surprising how, in that part of the world, there are these sudden drops, ascents and descents, that catch you unawares. Like the Granada, as it pulled out from behind us.

Suddenly it was there, big and menacing, grating its bulging metal side against the Volvo as it scrape-overtook in a sideways push powered by its 3-litre engine. I had one chance to look in the side-mirror as it came alongside, enough to make me freeze in horror; both sun visors were still down, obscuring the faces of driver and passenger but I caught very clearly the twin-rodded fingers of shine on the sawn-off shotgun the passenger was poking through his window. I couldn't veer right because the weight of the Granada was on that side. Stamping on the brakes I swerved left, hoping the hedge wasn't too solid.

It wasn't; but the ditch before it was deep enough for us to do a classic country roll, still at speed. One minute we were upright, hurtling into shrubbery, the next the nearside wheels gave way into nothing and the car went over on to its side, hovered for a moment, and then over on to its roof, squashing a hedge full of crackling twigs, innocent insects and birds' nests. Then it rolled over on to the other side, then it rolled over again. And again.

It's hard to describe what happened inside. My seat-belt snapped tight like a parachute harness, clamping me immobile. Pieces and things rained up and down as we circled over. Sue screamed, not loudly, more in

114

surprise than terror. Darkness succeeded light succeeded darkness again. My leg hit a knob under the dashboard. Cassettes rattled across the windscreen. The noise seemed deafening. Light flooded back again. We were upright but leaning sideways, down on Sue's side. I glanced towards her and congealed. We were poised on the brink of a much steeper slope, teetering over to her. The green meadow fell away at a sharp angle like the side of a Swiss ski slope. I hurled my door open, trying to counter-balance things as I yelled at Sue, grabbing her.

'Seat-belt!' I shrieked.

Fortunately, although she was rattled and shaken—she'd been turned upside down three times—she punched the release button like a wartime pilot with his engine on fire. Holding her tightly with my left hand, I freed myself and pulled all our weight to the right-hand side. Understanding, she clambered over the gear lever as the car gave a shiver and the two of us fell out of my door on to the grass, Sue on top of me as I held her.

The car rolled over again, away from us, quite slowly at first. Then, in front of a bunch of curious watching sheep, it rolled again, faster, and again, gathering speed. A door flapped open, swinging above the bulk of the car like a free flail on an agricultural implement. Bits of turf and mud flew up around the heavy gyrating mass of banging, impacted metal. At the bottom of the field, upside down, it stopped, exposing its dirty underside plates and wheels in a way that was powerfully shocking, like seeing a skirted matron doing a handstand. There was a smell of petrol.

The fire started slowly and there was no explosion. It spread quite deliberately, quite inexorably, bright and hot, from the front to the back until the whole car was steadily burning in front of us and the passing motorists who'd stopped and run into the field to see what on earth was happening. We stood there in a bunch with the sheep, watching my car, with its older memories of

Wittersham and Hastings and elsewhere, burn itself out into a hot metal shell.

CHAPTER 15

'An extremely nasty accident?' Nobby Roberts glared at me. 'Some accident! My foot!' He waved in the direction of Sue, who was sitting up in bed supported by pillows, looking very fetching in a flowered bedjacket. Apart from a bruise on one cheekbone there was nothing immediate to suggest she had been involved but I knew of bruises and scratches elsewhere, particularly on one slender leg. Rest all day Sunday had helped her a lot; she had sent me out to the Tate for the pile of books that reposed beside her but she had promised not to open them until now. Monday morning had arrived with a vengeance.

Nobby did a turn up and down the bedroom and came back face to face with me. His eyes matched his red sandy hair.

'I ought to run you in,' he snarled. 'I don't give a bugger about you, but Sue—well—you had no bloody business involving her at all.' He turned to her. 'You ought to throw this bastard out.'

'It is my flat,' I demurred mildly.

'That doesn't matter! Actually, Sue, Gillian says you *must* come and stay with us till you're better. Can you come now?' He glanced at me savagely. 'Before this fool gets you killed.'

'*Dear* Nobby. You are so kind. And Gillian too. But—'

'But nothing! I can't think why you bother with him! He's nothing but trouble! It'll come to a bad end! He won't listen to advice; he won't be warned. And you're too nice a girl to get involved.'

'Now see here, Nobby,' I said, still reasonable. 'There's no need to go off the deep end. And by the way you're not Sue's brother or uncle or something. There was no foretelling what happened. I—'

'That doesn't matter either! I feel personally responsible! I encouraged you two to get together again when Sue came back from Australia. I thought Sue would be a good influence on you. I wish I hadn't now! It—'

I grabbed him by the jacket lapels and heaved his face into mine. 'Nobby! This is me, remember?' I was shouting now. 'Tim! Remember me? We played rugger together at College. And afterwards. I helped you. You've got a bloody short memory, you have. Who got promoted at Scotland Yard after a certain affair in Brighton? What about that?'

'Boys, boys!' Sue's teacher-voice cut into my ears. I had a sneaking suspicion she was enjoying herself by having two grown men wrangle over her in the bedroom. 'Really! Stop it at once!'

He stepped back as I released him and brushed his lapels straight in fury. 'Certain affair in Brighton, indeed. I'm surprised that you have the gall to raise that subject here.'

I'm very fond of Nobby and his old-fashioned virtues so I smiled at him as I said, 'Sue knows all about the Godwin sideboard affair, Nobby. All about it. It happened while she was away in Australia and it's part of the past. You really don't think I wanted to risk Sue's life now, surely, did you?'

'Well, you have!' His voice was accusatory. 'No matter what you say, that's precisely what you have done! It's absolutely reprehensible of you!'

I caught Sue's eye. There was a faint sparkle in it so I gave her a stronger look, taking in her soft brown hair and her full mouth with a reproof that she responded to right away.

'Dear Nobby. Come and sit here.' She patted the side of the bed.

'Eh?'

'Sit here. Come on. I have a confession to make.'

He sat very gingerly about two feet from the point she'd patted. He looked like a dog that is not sure whether it is about to get a bone or a boot in the ribs.

'What confession?'

118

She gave him a soft appealing look that would have melted solid ice. 'It's all my fault. I insisted on being with him. Tim had no choice in the matter. I put my foot down.'

'I—you—you insisted on getting involved in this business?'

'Yes.'

'Knowing how he gets into—into—'

'Of course! Because of that! I'm Tim's partner now. I'm not letting him run off into these possible entanglements without me.'

'But look here, Sue, there could be very dangerous people involved. You have no idea what can happen. I'm a policeman: if I were to tell you one quarter of what happens you'd be terrified. Really you would.'

'I know. That's why I insisted originally that Tim brought you into things. He wouldn't have on his own, now would he?'

Nobby gulped. He shot me a furious glance. 'He certainly wouldn't. Do you know—'

'So that's why it's all right.' Sue's voice, interrupting, was soothing. She pointed at the books around her. 'I've a lot of research to do on family background. We're all going to work together. To find the awful people who killed that sweet old man.'

'Oh no we're not! Absolutely not!' He shot up stiffly, and stood erect, the formal Chief Inspector again. 'This is a matter for the police!' He wagged a finger straight at her. 'Only the police! You two are officially warned! Stay out of this! Christ! I'm going before things get any worse!'

He stamped out of the bedroom and I followed him cautiously through the living-room to let him out at the front door. His face was set as he looked at me. 'You're perverting that girl! It's a disgrace!'

'Calm down, Nobby. She's a strong-willed woman. Ask Gillian when you get home; she'll put you right. I stand no chance of keeping her out of it at all.' I lowered my voice. 'See the books? I got them for her yesterday from her office library at the Tate. It'll keep her occupied for days. By the time she wades through that lot you'll have the whole thing over. Trust me.'

His face eased a bit. 'You mean—she'll have to read through all those? Why?'

'Don't you remember what old Harwell said to us before he was murdered? It's a family matter, he said. The exact words were, "These people say that they are from his family." He said that to us when we were trying to calm him down after the first attack. "His" family. Sue thinks that he meant Whistler's family. Someone from Whistler's family or a descendant branch of it, trying to get the paintings. By threat. For all we know they may have got the paintings—and old Leonard Harwell—already. He's not been seen for a month at that shop in St Leonards. So it may be too late anyway; God knows what poor old Harwell might have had to tell them before he was killed. Anyway, Sue wants to research into family background. It can't do any harm and it'll keep her in bed, away from danger.'

'H'm.' I knew for a fact that Nobby, being a man of action, would see no use in bookish research of that sort. Clues, forensic science and hard work were the foundation of Nobby's professional life. He looked more mollified. 'I suppose it'll do no harm.' His face tensed up a bit once more. 'I had no idea that Sue was a keen interferer in these matters as well. God knows I've enough trouble with you; to have you paired up with another amateur shamus is a recipe for real disaster.' He stuck a finger under my nose.

'Keep out of the way, Tim. I'm warning you. Johnson is suspicious enough as it is; he's got a long memory.'

'So tell him to solve the case, quick, while she's doing her reading.'

He slammed the door so hard I thought that the knocker would fall off.

CHAPTER 16

Sue was sitting up in bed, holding a sheaf of paper. Books were piled around her and on the floor. She peered at me over the top of her hornrims as I handed her a glass of gin and tonic. I took my own Scotch and soda to the bedroom armchair, drank a swig from it, sat down and loosened my shoe-laces. She looked very pretty, sitting there dishevelled in a bedjacket, with the blankets up to her waist.

'Did you have a nice day?' she demanded, twitching the corner of her mouth at the implied Americanism.

'Regular, business-wise.' I took another sip from my glass. 'The lean Mr Casey sends his regards.'

She gave me a mock-flutter of the eyelids. 'Are you going to do business with him? Will I see him again?'

'Possibly.' The meeting had gone well. Andy Casey had been presented with a set of proposals covering the way we thought we'd work and he hadn't reacted particularly strongly against any of the main costs—yet. He was calm, professional and thorough. There was a lot to be said for him. Only one thought, a sort of sludge-residue from our evening together the previous Friday, kept stirring at the bottom of my mind. When we first met he'd said he associated me more with art and antiques than with railroad deals. Yet on Friday he'd said that James recommended him to Jeremy and his henchman called Simpson. It puzzled me; did he perhaps think, before, that there were two different Simpsons? It's a common enough name, so I supposed that was it, yet something nagged me, there in the sludge at the bottom of my brain.

Sue was staring at me. 'You're so forthcoming this evening. Do you want to hear what I've been doing?'

'Of course.'

'Where would you like me to start?'

'At the beginning.'

121

She compressed her lips. Her eyes gave me a short, intense stare, then she adjusted the hornrims and moved the sheaf of papers into position. 'I started with the Winanses,' she said, 'since Charles gave you that lead about Goldsworth and his client, and poor old Harwell said something about family. It seemed to be the most obvious place to go from.'

'Agreed.'

She shuffled the papers. 'It started with Ross Winans. The locomotive and carriage works, I mean. He was born in Sussex County, New Jersey, in 1796.'

'How appropriate.'

'Why?'

'Hastings and St Leonards are in Sussex. Sorry. An irrelevance. Go on.'

'He married twice, he sold horses to the Baltimore and Ohio Railroad in 1828, he had five children, he was a famous loco engineer as you know, he retired in 1860, he sided against the North in the Civil War, was arrested twice and released. Died in 1877. His wife was Julia De Kay, his first wife, that is. The second was called West. Elizabeth West. There were three children who really matter to us.'

'Good. Go on.'

'Julia, Thomas and William L. The key figure is probably Thomas, called Tom for short, certainly the most important historically. He was the energy in the firm of Harrison, Winans and Eastwick, formed to handle the Russian contract. He went to St Petersburg in 1843 when Whistler's father needed the firm to start building the locomotives and rolling stock for the Moscow railway. Actually Winans was added to Harrison and Eastwick at Major Whistler's instigation.'

'I know. It was a hell of an enterprise. They took on mechanics from everywhere, including a Glasgow boilermaker called Richard Smith who founded Smith's Boiler Works in Moscow. Sorry; that's another digression.'

She rustled her papers impatiently. 'Thomas left his brother William L. in charge in 1851 and returned to Baltimore, where he was still a director of the Baltimore and Ohio. He was recalled to Russia in 1866 for a new contract but the whole works was taken over by the Russian Government in 1868 and the firm was lavishly compensated. Actually, it was Tom Winans who bought Whistler's painting of Wapping in 1867 and took it to Baltimore.'

'I know. The Winanses made a fortune. Poor old Major Whistler died with no money in about 1849 and the family had to struggle. They estimated that the Winanses had made two million dollars as early as 1854 and they set up a vast house in Baltimore called Alexandroffsky after the loco works in Russia. Whistler's family got nothing out of Russia.'

'Not directly maybe, but George Junior did.'

'He did? How?'

'Well, that's the connection! George Whistler junior— our artist Whistler's elder half-brother—married Julia Winans.'

'Did he now? Very wise of him.'

'George was a bit of a problem to the family when young. He didn't join them in Russia and he had bad health so couldn't seem to settle to anything. He went to the South Seas of all places to recover and ate baked dog.'

'Christ.'

'I know. He said it tasted just like pig. Anyway, his parents were thoroughly glad when they heard the news that Ross Winans, out of business gratitude to his father, had taken George as a partner in the loco works in Baltimore. George seemed to settle then and had the good sense to marry Julia Winans. For a while, you see, I think they feared he might turn out to be like his uncle, William McNeill.'

'Who's he?'

'The brother of Whistler's mother, Anna McNeill. He surveyed the original line of the Baltimore and Ohio. He and Whistler's father were professional colleagues on that—after all, Whistler's father laid the first mile of track, after he'd been over to England in 1827 to talk to George Stephenson about the Stockton and Darlington Railway.'

'What was the matter with McNeill? Why did they fear that young George might turn out like him.'

She tilted her glass, emptied it and held it out to me. 'The demon drink. He took to it. Spent his life grumbling about missed opportunities and sponging on Whistler's father for money.'

I took her glass, remonstrating. 'But hang on, hang on! George and Deborah Whistler were the children of the first wife, Mary Swift. George had no blood relationship with Anna and William McNeill. Anna was simply the father's second wife, the one who had Jimmy and William, and a few others who died.'

'Yes, I know; but William McNeill was an Awful Example, wasn't he? Anna was a fierce Presbyterian and her brother's doings upset her terribly.'

'OK. Look, before I get you another, can we finish off the Winanses? I'm losing track—what a pun. We'd got to George Whistler junior marrying Julia Winans. What then?'

'Well, nothing really. They got terrifically rich. I read all about the Alexandroffsky house in Baltimore—very grand.'

'But Charlie Benson said that one of them had an estate in England, complete with footmen in Russian livery and carriages. Which one was he?'

'Ah, he must have been Walter. The son of William L. Like Jimmy Whistler, he was educated in Russia only much more so; he was an American citizen but he didn't visit America until he was fifty-eight. He wasn't in the business as far as I can tell. He wrote books on shooting.'

'Shooting? What kind of shooting?'

'Pistols, revolvers, sporting guns, that sort of thing. A rich man's interests. Shotguns among them, I suppose. She shot me a significant glance.

'So where is or was his estate in England and what family remains of his?'

'That's the odd thing. I can't find any. I phoned up a girlfriend of mine at Westminster Reference Library and she looked him up in *Who Was Who*. There's no record of any marriage or children.'

'What was his address then? We could go to the estate and find out.'

She sighed. 'He died on August 12th, 1920. There's no English address; the address given is the Carlton Hotel, Avenue de Tervueren, Brussels.'

'Shit. End of trail?'

'End of trail. In Belgium.'

I stamped out into the living-room and replenished both our glasses with some extravagance. The saga of the Winanses would have been an excellent lead if only we could have found some residue in England. I conceived what a tangled trail we'd have to follow if we had to track down all the remaining Winans relatives in America without being able to go there. It wasn't a hopeful prospect; there could be thousands of them.

Sue accepted her second gin and waited for down again. 'Actually I think that the Winans connections are much more important to the story of the artist James Whistler than people have realized or he himself would have cared to admit.'

'Really? Why?'

'Think about it. Jimmy left America in 1855 never to return. Half-brother George was already at the works in Baltimore and his younger brother Willie worked part-time there while studying medicine. Jimmy was star-struck by the idea of being an artist-student in Paris, particularly after failing at West Point. He'd read

Murger's book, *Recollections de La Vie de Bohème* from cover to cover and it was like *Star Wars* to a modern child. Without support from George or Tom Winans he couldn't have done it.'

'Maybe. But that was early days. Afterwards—'

'Afterwards,' she interrupted, 'it was the wealthy Tom Winans who acted as a sort of patron to Jimmy. Who bought the oil painting of Wapping? How on earth did Jimmy Whistler survive? Tom Winans lent him money, that's how.'

'Well, he didn't really survive that much, did he? He was always in debt. Went bankrupt after the Ruskin trial and that house in Tite Street.'

'There you are!' She was almost triumphant. 'Whistler always lived way beyond his means, like his chum Oscar Wilde. But at least Wilde made big money from time to time. Whistler was lavish to friends and acquaintances. His house was always full. Even when he was selling paintings to patrons like Leyland he can't have made that much. How on earth could he have commissioned an expensive Tite Street house to a special design from his friend Godwin? It cost two thousand pounds! Double what he got for the Peacock Room which cost the earth to do, and exactly what Tom Winans's estate claimed from him as owing when Winans died.'

'He meant to start an art school in Tite Street. Perhaps he thought that would pay for it.'

'Wishful thinking. I think that his allowances from George and Tom Winans kept him going. Mind you, he didn't want to tap George for a loan when George was dying in Brighton in 1869, but—'

'Eh? Brighton? For God's sake, how did Brighton get into this? George junior was in Brighton?'

'Oh yes. It was the weakly George who negotiated the contract-break settlement of the Russian business. The firm got five and a half million roubles from the Russian Government. George took sick on his way back and went to Brighton to recover en route. He invited them all—

Jimmy, Willie, mother and family—down there for Christmas but he died on December 23rd. Russia never seemed to do the Whistlers much good.'

'Bloody hell. Brighton and Hastings and London. George and Anna and Jimmy. I wonder if any of them bought a sideboard off Godwin?'

'Oh really, Tim! Please don't start any more red herrings! What I'm trying to say is that we don't know, but it is likely that the Winanses, particularly Tom and George's widow Julia, may have supported Whistler while all the time he was snobbing about as a grand artist and aristocrat. You couldn't live like Whistler without some sort of allowance, not until you married into the Philip family, perhaps.'

'The debt that art owes to steam locomotion is tremendous,' I said portentously. 'Turner would have agreed about that.'

She gave me another exasperated look. 'You and your ideas about art patronage! I give up.'

'Art is a rich man's indulgence, but let's not go into all that again. My head is throbbing with these Winanses. Can we go over the Whistlers themselves and see if there are any leads there? After all, that's what poor Harwell may have meant.'

'Certainly.' She started ticking them off on her fingers. 'Grandfather John you know all about. Anglo-Irish, private soldier at Saratoga, married Anne Bishop, back to America, Captain in the American army, founded Fort Dearborn, moved to Detroit during the war of 1812, had fifteen children of whom three went into the Army via West Point. Died in Bellefontaine, Missouri. Son George Washington Whistler born Fort Wayne in 1800, married Mary Swift, had George and Deborah, poor Mary died saying her friend Anna McNeill should take over, so George Washington Whistler obliged. Anna has James and William. All right so far?'

'All right, all right. There must be rafts of Swift and McNeill relatives in America, not to mention all the

127

offspring of the others, the Whistler uncles and aunts left out of the fifteen?'

'Of course. And Anna McNeill Whistler had relatives over here, in Preston. Winstanleys, they were.'

'Crumbs. We'll be on the road to Wigan pier next. Go on.'

'George junior we've dealt with along with the Winanses. Deborah married Seymour Haden and lived in Sloane Street. You know all about that?'

'Of course. Haden was a doctor but he became a famous etcher himself. He helped young Jimmy at first but then Jimmy became jealous of him and disliked his pompous moral lectures about Jimmy's way of life, particularly with Jo Hiffernan, so he pushed Haden through a plate glass window. Aggressive little rooster, Jimmy Whistler was. Prone to outbreaks of physical violence.'

Sue gave me an old-fashioned look and took off her glasses. 'That was all about something entirely different. Something more in your line of biographical memoir.'

'What?'

She grinned. 'Seymour Haden had an assistant called Traer, who was Whistler's personal doctor. Haden and Traer and Jimmy's brother Willie, who was now practising medicine in London, all went to Paris to a medical conference, during which Traer died. While visiting a brothel.'

'Tut-tut! Shocking!'

'Quite. Well, Haden hushed the whole thing up by having Traer buried very quickly without advising his family. The Whistler brothers remonstrated with Haden; relationships between him and Jimmy were always pretty tense. Jimmy shoved him and Haden went through a plate glass window. End of relationship with his brother-in-law. Whistler ended most of the relationships he had one way or another but usually with verbal violence rather than physical.'

'With a few notable exceptions. Legros, for example. That was to do with the way Whistler treated Jo Hiffernan when he came back from Valparaiso. She and Legros were models for the Wapping painting: I remember that now. But it was her nude pose for Courbet that made Whistler break with her; he was upset by that, just as he was about William Stott's painting of Maud later.'

'Ah.' Sue gave me another look. 'Speaking of nudes upsetting him, I've been tracing possible relatives from the—er—other side of the blanket. You see, while he lived with Jo he had an illegitimate son called John Hanson, who became a sort of secretary to him later. He used to refer to the boy as "an infidelity to Jo" because he was the result of an affair with another model. Then it's almost certain Jo had a child. And Maud Franklin probably had two, both daughters, in Paris. Certainly she had one daughter in Paris and came back to live with Whistler just off the Fulham Road—' she flashed me another significant glance — 'afterwards.'

'My God. So there are possibly a few descendants of those about?'

'Chelsea could be full of them. I mean, these are just the well-recorded ones or, rather, the, um, known ones, should I say. Whistler was devoted to La Vie de Bohème in his youth and had a cavalier attitude to women even if his manners were those of a gentleman. He regarded himself as an aristocrat, so poor Jo Hiffernan and Maud Franklin might call themselves Mrs Abbot or Mrs Whistler but they knew he would never marry them. Trixie Godwin was entirely different; she came of good family—the Philips— and was seen to be respectable, so he married her. Actually he was very fond of her.'

'Lucky girl,' I said drily. 'They didn't have any children, but of course there is another whole raft-full of relatives from the Philip side, presumably in Scotland?'

'Of course.'

I put my head in my hands. The only consolation, I thought, was that this ever-expanding pyramid of Whistler relatives would keep Sue occupied, but as though reading my thoughts, she took off her glasses and shuffled her papers together. 'That's that, Tim. I'm done with my research. I'll be glad to get out of bed and get going again.'

'Eh? Surely not? There must be much more to go through yet.'

'No.' She wagged a finger at me. 'Don't think you'll keep me tucked away here while you gad about. I've gone through the whole lot.'

'Look,' I said, thinking desperately, 'there must be other leads.' A brilliant thought struck me. 'What about Charles Augustus Howell? What about him? I mean, old Leonard Harwell appears to be calling himself Howell. That must be significant in some way, surely?'

Sue stopped shuffling the papers. Her face went serious. 'Charles Augustus Howell was an extraordinary entrepreneur and a swindler. Whistler called him "criminally an artist". He could steal and sell anything. He was secretary to Ruskin until Ruskin found him out and then he set about cheating Rossetti and then Whistler. He'd hoodwink anyone but they all liked him for his conversation and, of course, the women around him. He was massively promiscuous. His real value to Whistler was in selling etchings and paintings despite the fact that he pocketed a lot of the proceeds himself. He looked after John Hanson for Whistler too. The Rosa Corder you mentioned in the pub was one of his mistresses and was a minor painter herself. She was one of the few sitters who told Whistler that his portrait of her was finished and to stop fiddling with it.'

'I know,' I said absently, thinking of Rossetti. 'What happened to Howell? In the end, I mean.'

Her face was still grave. She paused before speaking and her voice wasn't quite under control. 'They found

130

him in a gutter outside a Chelsea public house. With his throat cut and half a sovereign in his clenched teeth.'

'What? Half a sovereign? You mean like—like—-'

'Like fifty pence.'

I stood up and leant against the door-jamb. What with all the relatives and their connections, my head had been swimming already. Now this macabre revelation. I stared back at Sue who, despite what she'd just said, was still looking very fetching in a rumpled sort of way. I needed to think.

'You're doing absolutely no good in there,' I said. 'The whole issue is giving me a headache. Come on, get dressed and come out; I'll buy you dinner at the trattoria round the corner.' Her jaw dropped. For a moment I thought she was going to expostulate, still surrounded by books and papers. Then she tucked the hornrims into a case and turned to me. 'Tim Simpson, you *have* changed! That's the first time since I've known you that you've ever asked me to get *out* of bed!'

I chuckled, but she'd already hopped out and disappeared into the bathroom. I filled up my glass again and brooded on the ritualistic aspect of old Harwell's murder. Had someone really known about the death of Charles Augustus Howell and half-repeated it? Surely not; it must have been coincidence, an accident. A modern fifty-pence piece bears no relation in value to a Victorian half-sovereign. But it is half of a pound. A sovereign pound. I shook my head. There were enough strong muscular hares in the list of relatives and connections Sue had compiled to chase across distant fields forever and now this: a possible ritual. It was enough to clog the mind of anyone.

The hi-fi was near me and I switched it on, idly thumbing through some records while I waited for Sue. My mind wasn't working properly. Some light music, rock, no, not classical, I thought, perhaps jazz. The record sleeves flicked past, some of them early stuff: Morton, Johnny Dodds, Omer Simeon. Then it hit me.

The first number on one of the LPs was an old 1920s jazz standard celebrating two streets: 29th and Dearborn. Dearborn. I stared at the title in apprehension, hardly noticing Sue's triumphant entry into the room, clad in jeans.

As anyone should know, Fort Dearborn is to Chicago what the Tower of London is to London. And Sue had reminded me, just a little earlier, that Captain John Whistler built it.

CHAPTER 17

'The Granada,' said Nobby Roberts irritably, his voice full of edgy telephone-tension, 'was owned by a greengrocer. We found it in Catford. It was stolen last Friday afternoon. Description fits, scrape along the side fits, last three numbers of licence which you obligingly remembered, also fit. It seems that this is the car. And that therefore we are dealing with professionals. Professionals, as a rule, do not re-enact strange, obscure murder rituals connected with half-Portuguese art dealers of the late nineteenth century. Professionals steal cars, the right cars for the job, and then ditch them. Professionals do the job, pinch the loot, kill the target and scarper. They do not place fifty p. coins in the teeth of dead men. Forget it, Tim.'

'There might be two different crews after the Whistlers, then, one pro, one amateur. Think of that.'

'There might be one hundred crews. It might be Cowes bloody regatta. So far the evidence points to one—a professional one.'

'Well, even supposing they didn't leave the fifty-pence piece and that it fell there by accident, what about the throat-cutting bit? After the poor old blighter had been bashed up?'

His voice modified. 'Look, Tim, they probably boobed. We don't know. If they got the pictures they almost certainly did him in. If one of them was a knife merchant he seems to have unknowingly done his nasty work after they killed Harwell by blows. Johnson's theory is that they killed him by accident while knocking him about. Then they ransacked the place. Then one of them finished him off just to make sure. It's fanciful, Tim, fanciful; the connection between Whistler and this dealer Howell and the way Harwell died —forget it! Who's ever heard of it?'

'A Whistler fanatic would have. If those two paintings are genuine, they're enough to get a real Whistler fan into a state of feverish excitement.'

'Murderous feverish excitement? That's stretching it a bit. No, Tim, these are pros. The real thing. It's all to do with money.'

'Well, they can't have found the paintings yet because they wouldn't have come after me and Sue otherwise, would they? There's still reason to believe that old Leonard Harwell holds the key—I take it you haven't found him yet because you'd have told me if you had?'

'No, we haven't. But we're concentrating on that area you suggest. Door to door. It takes time but we will find him this week, I'm sure of that.'

'There's a square mile of bedsits and flats. You'll have to put more than the local PC Plod on to it.'

'Don't tell me how to allocate resources! Do you know how many cases are on hand? Eh? Have you heard about the drug problem in South Coast towns?'

'All right, all right! Don't lose your wool. It was clever of you to locate the Granada so soon. I'm not complaining.'

'I should think not! This is no business of yours anyway.' His voice modified again. 'I'll tell you something, Tim: that Granada had every luxury you can imagine. It's incredible. Four-track stereo, electric windows and seats, heating, even air-conditioning, TV, cocktail cabinet, you name it. It must have cost a fortune. Bloody greengrocer could afford it; I'm a senior police officer and I couldn't.'

'Ah, well, there you are, you see, Nobby. You are a highly-respected civil servant and a moral force. We look up to you. The poor greengrocer is merely a business man. He has to have some compensations and—'

The phone came down so hard that I nearly burst an eardrum. Poor old Nobby; he's always leading with his chin. I grinned wrily at the portrait of George Melly painted by John Bratby on the wall eight feet away.

134

My office at the Bank is not exactly lavish; about eight feet by twelve and overlooking a tiled ventilation shaft in the middle of the block. I decided early on to put a few anarchic decorations into it so as to compensate for the feeling of wood-panelled mendacious gloom that accompanied the Bank's gravid operations. An extremely uncompromising female nude torso painted by Lucien Freud caused certain elderly secretaries to flinch visibly when they had to enter to deposit correspondence, and a gipsy circus scene by Munnings restored a certain philosophical balance to the view of life from a Bank. They often gave me satisfied consolation. Now I felt uneasy again. Jeremy had taken even more strongly to Andy Casey; Mary had apparently approved wholeheartedly of the healthy Chicagoan and his style. Jeremy could see kudos and international panache accumulating to him for a joint venture with Owens, McLeod and Casey over a deal in Brazil; his previous imaginings seemed to be dispelled by the security of James White's undoubted local expertise and our attention. I, on the other hand, found myself speculating on what else Casey was doing with his time in London; which US commercial banks, I wondered, and what for?

Before leaving for the Bank, while Sue was bustling about in the flat getting herself ready to go back to the Tate Gallery to work after her single day's absence, I surreptitiously sorted among my books and opened the Lippincott edition of the Pennell's *Life of Whistler* published in 1908. I found the passage I wanted quite easily:-

> According to Eddy, Whistler once said to a visitor from Chicago:
> 'Chicago, dear me, what a wonderful place! I really ought to visit it some day—for, you know, my grandfather founded the city and my uncle was the last commander of Fort Dearborn!'

Was it too fanciful, like the Howell connection with Harwell's death, to think that modern Chicagoans would want to own a Whistler for the original founding-grandfather connection? My problem is that, as Jeremy has often said, I have a mind full of stray biographical details, odd historical facts, mainly connected with art and artists, that warp my thinking and approach to objects and places. For instance, I can hardly walk down a London street without thinking of its past associations: people who met there, worked, lived in the houses, loved, fought and died there. It's a bad habit, distracting, apt to make you preoccupied with correlations that don't exist . . .

The telephone rang.

'Have you read *The Times* today?' Sue's voice was calm but full of meaning. 'Or have you only got the *Financial Times*, there at the Bank?'

'Hello, Sue.' I made it significantly courteous and warm, since she hadn't bothered to greet me. Doubtless she was at the back of the Tate, underneath, among the partitioned offices and the records, calm and professional and unartistic. 'We have both. I haven't read them. Why?'

'Have you got one nearby?'

'Yes.' I fished *The Times* out of an in-tray on the left-hand side of my desk. 'I have it here.'

'Try the Personal Column section.'

'For heaven's sake! I never read the—'

'Try it!'

With a shrug I turned to the inside back pages. 'What should I be looking for?'

'Under "Wanted". Have a look.' Her voice was short, peremptory.

It was half-way down. The name was printed in capitals. WHISTLER, it said, just like that. 'WHISTLER: paintings and etchings wanted urgently by American buyer. Best prices paid. Our client will be in England to

view. Please contact tel. no:—' A London number finished the ad.

'Christ!' was all I could say.

'It's in *The Times*, the *FT*, the *Guardian*, the *Telegraph*
and in the Sundays—I checked the old copies here.
What's more, three of this month's art and antiques
magazines are carrying it. So is the *Trade Gazette*.'

'Bloody hell.'

She let silence go by while I digested the news. 'I'd
better—'

'I've done it already. Phoned them, I mean.'

I felt helpless. 'Who is it?'

She was short, almost scornful. 'They won't say. Of
course they won't. It's an answering service. A girl. She
says if you give her details she'll pass the information
on. She's not allowed to give you the name of the client
or anything. She wants you go give your name and
address, then she says "they" will get in touch with you.
She doesn't even answer with the name of the answering
service company. Just the telephone number. It makes
me mad.'

'It's crazy. Who sells Whistlers that way?'

'Come on, Tim! Lots of people might; there are lots of
people who answer ads like that, for any old paintings,
furniture, silver. The papers and the mags always carry
them. Sometimes they list the artists by name,
sometimes they don't. Sometimes they get lucky. It's just
that it's very odd that particular ad being in the papers
right now.'

'Odd! It's bloody suspicious. I'll get Nobby to—'

'I've spoken to him.'

'Already?'

'Of course. Five minutes ago. He said he was talking to
you earlier.'

'Well, what did he say?' Huh, I thought, she phoned
Nobby before she phoned me.

'He says he can trace the number and he can find out
who's behind it. But he wasn't very keen.'

137

'Oh, for God's sake! Nobby is infuriating. Why not?'

'Because, he said, if you're going to knock off a Whistler or two and you don't care how you do it or who gets killed in the process, you don't draw attention to the fact by advertising yourself.'

'You mean he's going to do nothing about it?'

'Oh, he's going to make inquiries, pursue certain channels. *Very* defensive. D'you know, I think I've upset Nobby. What d'you think I've done? You've known him a long time.'

I grinned to myself at that. You've dropped the scales from his eyes, I thought, you've joined the Tim Simpson camp, you've told him to solve a case or you'll be cross, you're prying into police matters. But I said, 'Don't worry. He gets a bit shirty if you press him on any aspect of a case he's dealing with. He's probably narked because he didn't see the ad himself, not having time to read the papers thoroughly. He'll recover.'

'Well, what do you think?'

'Oh, I've more than a notion who's put that in. It's obvious.'

'Goldsworth?'

'It must be. Actually, it's probably time to have a chat to dear old Morris. When I've finished here, but before the galleries close, I think I'll pay him a visit.'

'Tim!'

'Just for a chat. Nothing personal. You know me.'

'I do! You are absolutely not to visit Goldsworth! It would be asking for trouble. What about Charles? He told you what he told you in confidence. It would ruin his position at Christerby's if you let Goldsworth know that you've been told he's after a Whistler. It's perfectly legitimate for him to advertise, if it is him, anyway.'

'He's a slimy bugger, that. I've never liked him. I ought just to—'

'Tim! Stop it! You leave everything to Nobby, do you hear? He'll have everything cleared up this week; he's said so and you know Nobby.'

'Indeed I do.' I was thinking of other cases. 'Very well. Let him get on. It's no skin off my nose.' I scowled at George Melly opposite; his violent impasto didn't stir.

'Thank heavens!' Her voice was relieved. 'You really are a liability. Your first instinct is to put your head down and charge. Just like a bull at a gate.'

'Mmm.' Something else had occurred to me.

'Tim? Have you been listening? When are you getting back this evening?'

The phone came back into focus. 'What? Oh, early. In fact, I want to see you, early. Outside the Tate at five? Bottom of the steps?'

'Wha—why? I can get home perfectly well with—'

'Be there, Sue,' I said sharply. She'd had quite enough of her own way, in my opinion. 'There's a good girl.' I had to add that, for insurance purposes; I'm a coward where Sue is concerned.

CHAPTER 18

I had already bought a Jaguar XJ coupé. Well, to be honest, I didn't actually buy it myself: the Bank did. It seemed time for a change and I got a very good deal on a slightly second-hand one with automatic transmission. As a concession to respectability it was black but somehow I felt it was the right sort of car for me, now. I drove round to the Tate Gallery and picked Sue up with it, just to show off. Dead on five, as I'd said; Sue nearly had kittens when she saw it.

'My gosh,' she chirruped. 'You *are* becoming a flash lad, Tim Simpson. Who were you hoping to pull with this machine? Come on, take me for a drive; I rather like the idea of swanning about in a sports.'

'It's no good for pulling birds, really,' I said, when we'd both got in. 'By the time you'd clambered over the transmission tunnel and caught your equipment on the stick, the target would have died laughing.'

Sue giggled, but I could see she was impressed. I shot across the end of Vauxhall Bridge and followed the Embankment past Chelsea Old Church and Lindsey House until we swung into Cremorne Road and on up to Earl's Court. Then I turned left on the Cromwell Road extension and we were soon on the M4, going like ten bells. It was late afternoon and warm, with a low sun in our eyes so that she leant back, half-lidded, humming to herself. From time to time she glanced across at me with a smile and shook her head slightly as though she'd got in tow with a hopeless case. I couldn't look at her for too long because I had to watch the road and keep an eye out for police cars—we were doing more than a hundred—but I could tell that the Jaguar had given her a sort of flush, a friction-rub to the system. There's something about change, pure change in itself, that stimulates people, particularly if it gives the impression of being for the better.

Actually the Jaguar had not cost much more than a new Volvo estate would have. I was deeply fond of the Volvo, I'd had good times in and with it, carrying antiques and girls whose memory gave me pleasure and sadness, but it was time to change. And, I'd reflected, Sue would probably see it as a new era, devoid of past associations, sort of 'our' car, for our new partnership. At least, that's what I hoped.

We cleared the tangle of London Airport and Slough with a flicked view of Windsor Castle. The turn-off to Maidenhead and the connection to the Oxford road were next. Then it was a pleasant flat-out trial, passing the filled gravel pits, the brewery, the flat land just south of Reading. From where we had left Hammersmith to the exit at junction twelve took me just about thirty minutes. Sue looked up in surprise as we left the motorway and I turned up the road north, to Pangbourne.

'Where are we going?'

'It's a surprise.'

This was very far from seedy old Hastings and St Leonards. Not so far in miles but very far in circumstances. We were coming to the prosperous old-world charm of the Thames valley of the City man, the successful stockbroker, the horse-owning international set. As we reached the warm red Tudor brick of Pangbourne I turned right and crossed the river, snatching a glance at the foaming weir, the green banks and fine houses. Just over, I caught sight of a steeple and found a lane through gateposts that led to a timbered lych-gate in front of the church. Sue raised her eyebrows.

'Whitchurch,' I said, clambering out. 'To be accurate, I suppose it's Whitchurch Church. Come on.'

The churchyard was grassy and empty from the gate to the double-roofed, flint-walled building with gothic windows. The steeple was a simple tapering spire set on to the square lower section by shorter bevels, like an upturned ice-cream cone of angular design. As we reached the door I wondered if I might have to fetch a key, but the church was open. I swung the heavy timber and we went into the empty building.

It was quite large inside, almost cavernous, and a bit gloomy. I found some switches and flicked them. Lights went on in the entrance area but not in the main body of the nave which was still mercifully light from the big western-end gothic window, giving a strangely yellow tone to the interior. I looked along the wall-tablets as I walked to the middle aisle, but, not seeing what I wanted, glanced down. I was standing on one of them. John Whistler, the big slab said, of the Manor of Whitchurch, died 1780. I squinted at the careful script engraved into the dark stone, worn smooth by the shuffling generations of worshippers. With him, the inscription said, the line went extinct. Well, that line maybe, but not the one I was dealing with; mine was a different line. I moved carefully down towards the altar, passing a William, who died in 1705, and two tiny children, Elizabeth and Mary, 1676 and 1696 respectively, only three years old. The floor was paved with dead Whistlers. I looked up to Sue's intent face as I reached the next tombstone.

'That's one,' I whispered, pointing. 'At least, I think it is.'

Ralph, the slab said, 1607—1696. Sue peered at it. 'Who's he?'

'The Ulster branch was founded by a Ralph. In the seventeenth century. The name fits, and the dates. This is possibly the root of our Whistler.'

Her eyes were wide; she shook her head gently from side to side. I passed on to a Thomas, died 1722, and to John and Henry, both young men, John died in 1690 aged 26 and Henry in 1698 aged 13. Then there was a resounding Latin Antonius and a Gilbert.

No more.

I searched about a bit further while Sue looked round the church. After she had seen all she wanted to she came up to me, her face strangely peaceful and rapt.

'What are you looking for?' she demanded.

'He's not here. We'll have to go to Goring.'

I took her hand and led her out, shutting the door carefully. We walked back in silence through the grass to the Jaguar and I took the road back over the bridge. Turning right, I followed the river past the cheerful Victorian Queen Anne brick-and-balconies of the Seven Deadly Sins and on up the well-ordered wealthy countryside to Streatley, where I turned right over the river, into Goring.

This time the lych-gate was much older, simpler, a sort of timbered open shed with a tiled roof trapped between garden walls. The asphalted path ran wide, down through many graves to the old humped church with ancient flint walls and a square tower. Above us green headlands reared their smooth meadowed shoulders high beside the river. There's a quality about the light and air up the Thames valley beyond Maidenhead that is hard to define; the noise of the river and the ambience lull the visitor into dreaminess. I glanced at Sue; she was taking it all in as though she'd never been there before but I knew she must have; three years at Oxford must have given her plenty of opportunity. Suddenly I felt jealous of all those undergraduates who must have taken her out, on the river, along the valley, round the regattas.

'Come on,' I said. 'Let's see if he's here.'

The church interior was smaller, simpler, with washed walls. There were few memorial tablets. When we got to the top, near the altar, I found the first: Hugh Whistler, son of Master John Whistler of Goring, departed this life the 17th day of January AD 1613 being aged what looked like 216 years but, on closer examination, turned out to be 46 years. There was also a Helinor and a Johannis and a Willi of Stapenhill and a Radulphus of

143

Fowlescote in Berkshire. More interesting, there was a very early brass of Whistlers dressed in Tudor-Elizabethan clothes, very grave and ruffed. I shook my head at Sue.

'Sir Kensington's not here,' I said. 'Perhaps he was the Essex branch. Or the Sussex one.'

She took my arm, hooking her hand into the elbow joint like one about to walk formally down the aisle after a ceremony. 'Tim, what are you doing? Who was Sir Kensington?'

'Tut-tut. You've read the books. He was the grand cousin who had the young John Whistler from Lough Neagh sent to the Americas. He's not here. I rather fancied finding him. Just for curiosity to mark the cause of it all. And for the drive; it was a nice drive, wasn't it?'

She shook her head in amusement and tightened the grip on my arm. I led her out into the churchyard surrounded by soft pink brick walls, the old houses and the weired river under the timber-joisted bridge supports. Slowly we walked up to the old lych-shed and I stopped to look back.

From here, from Goring and Whitchurch and this Thames valley area, the Whistlers had spread out all over the world. They went to Ireland and America and Russia. Soldiers and parsons, the books had said. There was much of these two traits in Jimmy Whistler; fighting and preaching. He had wanted both to play the pipes—that was what it meant, Whistler, a piper—and to call the tune. It couldn't work, not in his way. You couldn't be an artist, live La Vie de Bohème, cock a snook at respectable society and expect to be treated like a gentleman, full of hypocritical proprieties. If you were prepared to conform, be an RA, follow Johnny Millais, bow to society's totems, yes. But not if you lived like Whistler and scorned Victorian painting. All the affronts, the imagined insults, the biting remarks, the fury with English society, respectable, superficial, came from this inability. Whistler knew the weaknesses, the sins and vices of London and Paris. Compared with many, his life was lived in much more open honesty. What he said about art now seems obvious, clear, totally acceptable. In his lifetime it upset the boat. I thought of him, buried in Chiswick, and the other Whistlers dead in Detroit and Missouri, in Brighton, in Massachusetts, in Kentucky and Hastings and St Petersburg. It led me to think of my father, buried in Callão, and my mother, cremated in Bournemouth.

'What is it, Tim?'

'I was just wondering if, in x hundred years time, anyone will go looking for the root of the Simpsons.'

She put her head on one side and looked at me, sideways. The brown hair had fallen over one cheek and her body, slightly tilted by the movement, pushed an appealing hip towards me on the near side.

'You wouldn't consider, say, founding a Simpson dynasty with me by any chance, would you?' I asked it lightly enough, but I looked deep into her blue eyes.

Her face stilled gravely. She turned full-face to me and put her arms round my neck. Her voice was very gentle.

'I'm not ready for dynasties, sweetheart. You know what we agreed. I can't explain it; it's too soon for me. I know how it was for you when you were married and you've changed a lot since then. When I went to Australia I thought I'd never see you again, never bother with you, quite apart from believing you'd never see me. Sometimes I think how strange it is, our being together again now; sometimes I can't believe life has ever been anything else or ever will be. Can you understand? Everyone keeps telling me that I'm old, twenty-eight, I should settle down. Something different, inside me, tells me that life isn't just that, not any more, not for me. One day I'll know; trust me.'

She took her arms away and we walked back down the long old path to where the car shone low and shiny black in the closing evening light.

'It's a super car,' she said. 'I love speed: it's exciting. Come on, show me what it'll do on the way back.' She put her face close to mine as I bent to open her door for her. 'Then I'll show you what I can do,' she whispered, sweet in my ear.

I don't suppose I'll ever get a better offer than that, but somehow, afterwards, my memory preferred to avoid the quaint old lych-gate at Goring Church.

CHAPTER 19

I folded *The Times* carefully under my arm as I strolled up Bond Street from the Piccadilly end. Agnew's had an exhibition on; a light rain was starting to fall and I was tempted to browse in the entrance to get out of the drizzle. At half past four it was surprising how many of the people hurrying down the pavement were obviously getting away from work early. But then, like Whistler, I've always been a bit of a Puritan at heart; anything before five at the very earliest seems to me a guilty time to leave.

As I reached Morris Goldsworth's I hesitated: I began to think that the risk might not be worth it. Instincts were prevailing again; when I was a new, young business consultant I spent a lot of time doing market research, chatting people up, digging into statistics. Like an old dog, I was turning to old tricks. A bad conversation with a possible informant was better than no conversation at all. Morris Goldsworth might not be my favourite dealer, nor I his favourite rival, but we were in the same business, for the same raw material. We had to live together. I pushed the glassy door and went in.

The problem with galleries like Morris Goldsworth's is that they set my teeth on edge. The major part of his stock was aimed at names, not at art. Fashionable names, in long lists, are the stock-in-trade of men like Morris. And the paintings; I know a few daubers who could turn out most of Morris's stock monthly. It's a professional approach, of course; people don't want misery, storms, grey skies, poverty and depression. They want colour, flowers, happiness, pretty girls, sunshine, cheerful landscapes. I mean, bugger Art with a Capital A, you've got to *look* at the bloody painting when you get it home. What use is a meaningless splash twelve feet by ten when you live in a bijou Mayfair flat— or a South

Kensington flat, come to that—with only one full blank wall and no long vista to stand back and view from?

The first painting that caught my eye was a Terrick Williams of a Brittany harbour. I approve of that; Williams was a good painter, especially of those Brittany harbours with fishing-boats and people mending nets. It's a sort of foreign Newlyn school if you like, with clearer colours. The only problem was that Morris's restorer had floated the usual wash of cirrillian blue sky over the upper half to cheer up the colour a bit, just as all the eighteenth-century landscape dealers do. He'd turned up the contrast knob, too; heightened the lights, deepened the shadows. It made a more dramatic picture but it was no longer a Terrick Williams; it was a Morris Goldsworth's restorer's, whoever he was.

'Yes?'

The tall, soft, well-suited hooray henry stood across my path, head up, body tense, emanating hostility. His jaw was tight, making his lips protrude in a grimace of dislike.

'Is Morris in?'

His face contracted. The impression given was that one had asked a particularly unfortunate and uncouth question.

'I'm afraid not. Mr Goldsworth is not available just now.'

He didn't add anything that might have smacked of courteous service or interest, like Can I help you? or even What are you after? He just stood there, legs apart. I turned my gaze on to an undistinguished still life by Duncan Grant and sighed.

'Just tell Morris that Simpson would like a word, there's a good fellow, would you?'

His brow clamped into a scowl. He had a clean white skin of the thick type, slightly pasty, and very dark eyebrows over the brown pupils. He was going to have a blue chin in a few years' time.

'Mr Goldsworth is not available.'

148

Suddenly I felt sorry for Morris Goldsworth. It's all very well for people like me to bang on about paintings and keeping them pure; we don't have to run a Bond Street gallery. We don't have crushing overheads, employees, difficult customers. The works hanging on the walls were what people wanted, what Morris could sell. You could argue that he didn't *have* to be a dealer, didn't have to trade. It was just his living, that's all, trading in paintings, and the essence of any trading business is turnover. We could buy art and put it away; Morris had to move it on. My eye caught a Seago of flat Norfolk landscape; it looked vaguely familiar and I peered closer.

'Christ,' I said to the scowler, 'you've cut that down. I remember when it came up in the rooms; I nearly bid for it. It was bigger then; a huge sky, there was.' I moved nearer to it. 'You've sliced about three inches at least off the top and re-lined it, haven't you? To alter the proportion? More saleable that way, I suppose, because a big empty sky isn't so popular, but it's not Seago's work any more, is it?'

He didn't actually grind his teeth but his lower jaw moved in a clamped, muscle-bound sort of way. He took a step towards me.

'What do you want, Simpson?' A new voice spoke from behind him.

Morris Goldsworth is a big man, nearly six foot six, tapering from a forty-six-inch waist upward to a curly-haired head. He's about fifty and he wears huge spectacles with thick tortoiseshell frames to them, like a pair of brindled goggles. The lenses are not very thick but they give his eyes a frozen look and, when he moves, they jerk from one focus to the next so that it's hard to know what he's really thinking. His dark suit was open; his white shirt strained at the waistline and the buttons bulged their way up to a stiff collar. A dark-patterned tie lay on the sloping surface like a ladder on a church roof the only time it would ever swing free would be when he leant forward to inspect a canvas from close quarters.

'Hello, Morris. I thought you might be hiding at the back there. I wanted a quick word about the ad in *The Times.*'

His face didn't budge. The scowler stood still, waiting for his chief to move. Goldsworth stared at me in silence for nearly twenty seconds. 'What ad in *The Times?*'

I took the paper out from under my arm and handed it to him ready-folded at the Wanted column. 'Halfway down. The Whistler ad. It should be of interest to us both, surely?'

He put one hand on the big frames to steady his spectacles while he held the paper in the other. Impassively he read it and then handed it back. 'I've seen that elsewhere,' he said.

Quite a poker-player, our Morris. Dealers have to be. Give nothing away, show no interest, wait for the other side to commit themselves, blow the gaffe. 'An American customer,' I said, looking hard into the brindle-framed lenses. 'Looking for a Whistler. Seems to me that that's our territory, Morris, yours and mine.'

His face changed. 'Why? You haven't taken to dealing, have you, Simpson? Come in here to check on the prices, have you? What's an American buyer to you, anyway? You and your City funds; it's we dealers who make the market for you. You live off us. Bloody parasites.'

I cleared my throat. 'You don't think there may be aspects of this on which we might collaborate, Morris? A Whistler is something of interest to both of us.'

'Collaborate? With you? You must be joking—I'd rather collaborate with a tarantula. If White's Fund bought anything off me I'd know that I'd failed: it would be too cheap.'

'Steady now, Morris. There's no need to get unpleasant. It just seemed to me that—'

'Well, the answer's no!'

The big young man smiled.

'Look, Morris, I'm just trying to—'

'No!'

'Time to leave, Simpson.' The white soft face showed pleasure. 'You've heard what Mr Goldsworth said.'

I looked at him and then at Morris. 'What's this?' I demanded. 'The son of one of your financial backers? Taken the boy in to the fine art trade, have you, so that he can live like a gentleman?'

He took a step forward. Goldsworth practically shouted. 'Stop! Stop there! Simpson, you get out! You're not welcome here. We meet in the auction rooms and nowhere else. I'm not collaborating with you on anything. I don't want you snooping about in my gallery.'

'Let me throw him out.' The scowl was back.

'I bet you were good at games when you were at school, sonny.'

He bunched his fist and drew his arm back. Goldsworth let out a bellow. 'Don't be a bloody fool, Julian! Stand back! He'll massacre you. It's just what he wants. I'm not having violence here.' He turned to me. 'If you don't get out I'll call the police. Do you hear?'

'OK, Morris, I'm going; I'm going. There's no need to go into a flat spin. It was a perfectly reasonable request to make.'

'Not from you it wasn't.' He strode past me, wrenched the door-handle and opened up to the street. Then he stood stock-still, upright, stiff, waiting. I shrugged sadly and ambled past him. As I drew level the big soft Julian spoke.

'Don't come back.' The tone was triumphant, sneering, superior. For a brief moment I thought of replying, of dealing with him. Five years earlier I would have without question; before Sue came back I might have. Now I just shrugged again and left, hearing Goldsworth close the door behind me. A complete waste of time. About as much use as baiting a dog. Yet I wondered, as

151

I strolled down Bond Street; Morris was well-known for his readiness to deal, to get into cahoots with all sorts of people. Mainly in the trade, of course, but why not others? Money is money; when traders get a sniff of White's heavy bank balance their usual reaction is to play along for a while at least, just to see if there's anything to be gained. This was outright rejection: an absolute zero. I wondered if Morris had got on to a Whistler through his ad and was anxious to keep all possible invaders out or whether there was something deeper in it. That Morris regarded me with extreme dislike at the best of times didn't help. I decided I should have known better; I should have listened to Sue.

It was just after five. The pavements were crowded and public transport would be jammed. I managed to grab a taxi and sat back in it while it threaded its way towards South Kensington. The best thing I could do would be to head for home and say nothing to Sue. The whole business was out of my hands; it was ridiculous, my sniffing round Goldsworth like that. The taxi stopped outside the flat; I glanced at my watch. Sue wouldn't be home yet. Suddenly I changed my mind; other queries were pushing themselves into my mind and I needed to talk to someone. Sliding back the inner window, I spoke to the patient cabbie.

'King's Road,' I ordered. 'The Chelsea end.'

CHAPTER 20

The shop was shut. After half past five the sullen girl always left, banging the pots and pans behind her as she slammed the door. I'd missed her but I wasn't bothered. At the side of the shop, set in the terraced façade of houses, shops and alleyways, there was a door with a separate bell. It was placed at the end of a long internal passage leading down the side of the shop to another staircase, a narrow one, that went up to Charlie Benson's chapel. I leant on the bell and waited. The original purpose of the extra access was to meet the fire regulations; Charlie didn't use the side entrance that often, just as a sort of escape-route if customers he didn't want to meet came in the front way. An old fox, Charlie: when I lived in the Fulham Road I used to drop in on him quite regularly to chat of this and that.

It took a few minutes for sounds to come from behind the door. Then it swung open and Charlie's bushy black beard bristled suspiciously forth.

'Hello, Charlie. Sorry to bother you.'

'Tim!' The beard receded, softened, as the face lit up. 'Hello, mate! Come in, come in. What brings you here again?' He backed against the wall to let me past. 'Go on up; I'm playing with me little toys again. Come and talk to me while I fiddle. How are you?'

'Fine, thanks, Charlie.' I tramped up the narrow flight, feeling my way a bit; the inner staircase was dark, relying on a glow from the 'chapel' above. 'How are you?'

'Mustn't grumble. Had a bit of luck today.'

'Really?' The top door opened outwards so that the trestled platform around the big hall had to be set only slightly out to give visitors access. You had to duck under the layout on all fours to crawl to the middle and Charlie came grunting after me as I stretched upright, surrounded by the extensive landscape of diminutive railway England, all dinky buildings and pocket-size

153

carriages. He gestured at a china plant-pot in a china stand like a sort of deep dish. 'Look at that; feller comes in today and sells it me as Derby, see. Nice, ain't it?'

It was white, that old sort of white that two-hundred-year-old china gets, decorated with a painted pheasant in fine colours next to a humming bird on a plant. The stand had a butterfly painted on the side. 'Very nice,' I said cautiously. Porcelain is not my strong suit; there's too much of it.

He grinned. 'I gave him five hundred quid for that. Derby, I says, very nice, and off he goes.' His grin broadened. 'Only it's Chelsea Derby, see, not just Derby; around 1770, it is. Duesbury, that is, from Chelsea moulds, made by Chelsea workmen. I'll double the price when I sell it.'

His pleasure was infectious. 'You cunning devil, Charlie,' I said. 'You're a real Chelsea type.' Then I stopped.

On the floor, near the main door, propped against the wall, was an oil painting of a hazy Thames scene, late nineteenth century. Grey mist shrouded a wharf and a bridge with bluish overtones. The bridge was high, jacked up on wooden piers with open-beam structuring. Under it, in the distance, was a dark shoreline with occasional yellow pinpricks of light. There were figures on the bridge, stiff and stilted, painted by a man with little anatomical skill, like a primitive. It was a Whistler Nocturne, painted by someone else, less sure of themselves, less confident.

'Christ,' I said.

Charlie followed my gaze. His eyes crinkled. 'Ah, now then, Mr Art Expert, what's that? You tell me, eh? It isn't signed.'

'Walter Greaves.'

He slapped his thigh. 'Right first time! Ten out of ten! I can tell that living in the Fulham Road wasn't completely lost on you.'

I crossed the centre, ducked under six feet of rolling countryside, the London and North Eastern Railway's main line, four sidings, a tunnel and a quantity of sheep and cows, to emerge in the open space by the main door so that I could pick up the canvas and look closer at it.

'Poor old Walter Greaves. He did everything that Whistler did. Etchings, watercolours, oils. Whistler absolutely buggered his life up for him.'

'Pooh.' Charlie's voice was contemptuous. 'He should have stayed a boatman like his dad. That's all he and his brother were good for. Rowing Whistler up and down the river to help him do his sketching. That's what he employed them for. He didn't ask them to try and become painters like him. That was their lookout. So the family business went bust and Greaves ended up touting for business along the Embankment with his brushes. Paint anyone or anything for coppers, he would.' His face cleared again and a smile came back. 'Not that I'd sell that cheap, of course. Fetch money, his paintings do now.'

I held the painting carefully. I didn't want to argue with Charlie. Walter Greaves painted his father's boats as a lad, in fanciful patterns. Before he met Whistler he painted in the pure strong colour of a remarkable primitive. Whistler not only imposed his own low tones on him, he turned the Greaves brothers into nothing better than servants and then deserted them. Greaves was a simple, gentle man who suffered abject poverty after Whistler spurned him. He allowed himself to be dominated by Whistler, trusting him, helping him to paint the notorious Peacock Room. Peacocks are said to be unlucky; nothing went right for Whistler or for Greaves after the Peacock Room. Soon afterwards Whistler moved to the White House in Tite Street; Greaves was no longer wanted.

People have mistaken a few of Greaves's paintings for Whistler's because the influence was powerfully strong. As soon as the brothers started to show signs of branching out on their own, however, the shrill jealous verbal barbs were shot, as they were to Sickert, Wilde and countless others.

Whistler's possessive, insecure streak would allow no pupil to draw level, no acquaintance's light to shine with equal brightness. The West Point Cavalier had failed to fight in the Civil War for his tenuously-claimed Southern inheritance; the amoral bohemian believed powerfully in his mother's Puritanism; the brilliant painter-decorator had achieved no Royal Academy recognition, no secretly-coveted seal of approval for his position as a leader of fashionable taste. Whistler knew, deep down, that his place was ephemeral, he belonged nowhere; he needed adulation and his prickly antennae were ever alert for a hint of disdain or for local challenge.

'I'll give you a turn on it, Charlie,' I said amiably. 'Walter Greaves is part of art history.'

He shook his head. 'Nah. Not yet, Tim. I want to look at that for a bit. It's a bit of Old Chelsea, see: I'm a Chelsea boy and that's Battersea Reach. I mean, I think, like everyone did, that he should've stuck to his father's boatyard, that's my opinion. Whistler was the star; stars have to have their hangers-on, paint-mixers, dressers, the lot. The Greaves was just like, well, fans are nowadays to rock singers. They dressed like him, followed him, did everything he wanted. They shouldn't complain when he moved on.'

I chuckled. 'Whistler groupies, you mean?'

'Ha! Yeah, that's it. Whistler groupies.'

'Where did you get it, Charlie?'

He put a finger down the side of his nose. 'I have my methods, Tim. Local, it was. Nice and local, an all-Chelsea story. You know how it was; Greaves sold anything for a few bob, to make ends meet. Silly old bugger.'

I gave it another look. Just the sort of painting that someone, thinking it was Whistler, would dig out of the attic and present to a dealer, hoping for a fortune. In response to an advertisement, perhaps.

'Have you had it long?' I asked casually, fingering the edge of the chipped frame as I set it back on the floor, thinking, as I did so, how high the trestled bridge looked; out of proportion, like Whistler's worm's eye view of Old Battersea Bridge.

He gave a perfectly open set to his eyebrows, pulling his mouth down a little as he thought for a second or so. "Bout two weeks. It was here when you last came but I had it down in me office at first so I could see it. Brought it up here out of harm's way and so that bloody stupid foreign dealers wouldn't keep asking to buy it instead of the junk they deserve.' He grinned at me, dispelling any doubt that he'd acquired it before the ad came out. 'If I'd known you was keen on it I'd have showed it to you, but I thought you was only interested in railways.'

'I was, then. As a matter of fact, I came to ask you about another railway thing. You remember what you said about the Winanses? About the four-wheel end bogies on carriages that they invented?'

He picked up his tiny screwdriver. 'Yeah. I remember. It's an agreed fact. Why?'

'And their works was in Baltimore? Apart from the Russian thing, I mean?'

'Yeah.' He removed a front axle from a tank engine and put the two little wheels carefully into the Chelsea-Derby plant pot. 'This is going to be useful.' He grinned mischievously.

'A one-thousand-pound component bin. I like that. They didn't have any connection with Chicago, did they?'

His face puckered, making the beard bristle again. 'Nah. Not that I know of. Nor with Al Capone, neither.'

'Did Whistler's father?'

His face went blank. He shook it gently. 'Don't think so. He was the civil engineer, see? Surveyed the line,

157

built it, put up the bridges and embankments, laid the track. Organized the whole thing. The Winanses built the locos and the rolling stock with Eastwick and Harrison. They also supplied materials for bridges and track. To Whistler's spec, of course; he built the railroad and he knew a lot about locos. Didn't do Chicago, though. Baltimore and Ohio, that was him. A few others. Baltimore and Susquehanna. Paterson and Hudson. Providence and Stonington. Then there was that one— what was it—Western Railroad of Massachusetts? From Boston to Albany. That was the first through railroad of any importance, that was, in America.'

'Christ, Charlie, I didn't know you were an expert on early American railways too.' Albany, I thought, why does that ring a bell?

He chuckled drily. 'I'm not, much. But I do know about George and Robert Stephenson, see? And Whistler's father came over with his brother-in-law McNeill and someone else to see the Stephensons and study the railways here before they built the Baltimore and Ohio. He was an admirer of George Stephenson's, was Whistler's father. He played around with Stephenson's models when he worked in Lowell for the Booths. That's where Jimmy Whistler the artist was born; in a northern manufacturing town, not the South, like he claimed.' He pointed his little screwdriver at me. 'I'll tell you something else not many people know either, Tim. Whistler's father painted too. There's one of his showing Detroit as it was in 1820.'

'Go on.'

'There is. I've seen it in a book somewhere. So you could say it was all in the family; the painting, I mean.'

'Yes.' I scratched my chin. 'Talking of paintings, Charlie, you know that Morris Goldsworth is advertising for a Whistler?'

He let out a sort of rip-snort that convulsed the bulky frame and jerked his arm, dropping the screwdriver. 'Morris Goldsworth! That bloody—that bloody—' he snuffled about the floor, grunting with effort—'that bloody Bond Street bastard! Him and his so-called backers!' The screwdriver pointed at me again. 'He was a Chelsea boy, he was, Tim. Did you know that? I bet you didn't. Well you wouldn't, would you? Eh? Smooth effing idiot with those effing tortoiseshell gig-lamps and a voice gone all plummy. From here, he was. I can remember when Morris Goldsworth was a runner, I can. Knocking from door to door and spying from shop to shop. Used to run for three or four of them, he did. Harwell was one. Bastard: got himself some burke with money to back him and off he went. I threw him out of here once. Tried to beat me down on a price on a drawing by Augustus John. Said it might not be genuine. I knew it bloody was; John gave it to the tart who posed for it, after he'd had her. And she sold it to me. Years afterwards, mind, when she needed a bob. A sketch it was, part of a study for something else. He had a studio in Manresa Road, just up the way, then. I says to Goldsworth, I knew this trade when you was a snot-nosed runner, I says, and I know more than you'll ever know, I says. Out you go. 'E scarpered quick, I'll tell you.'

The powerful body trembled in resentment and his eyes glared. If I'd been Goldsworth I'd have exited pretty smartly, too. I'm not weak but I wouldn't fancy tangling with Charlie, not in one of his rages.

'He's not one of my favourites either,' I said.

His frame relaxed a bit. He bared his teeth. 'I've heard that. I was glad to hear you upset him a few times, just when he thought he'd got a snip.'

'Yes. Well, we may tangle more substantially one day.' Albany, I suddenly remembered, something to do with Casey. What the hell was it?

'Nothing new about the poor old Harwells, is there, Tim?'

'Eh? Oh the Harwells. No. Nothing. They haven't found the brother yet but they will. Somewhere in St Leonards. Shouldn't take long.'

159

'Good.'

'Nothing's turned up yet. Of the Whistlers, I mean.' A thought occurred to me. 'No one's tried to offer you any Staffordshire, have they, Charlie? Along with the Chelsea- Derby?'

'Nah.' He chuckled. 'None of that.' He moved to a control panel.

'There was a very pretty figure of a gardener, early one it was, standing with a shovel and a basket of flowers or fruit. They've not found that.'

He pressed a button and an engine twitched in a siding. 'No? Have they put out a description?'

'No. That reminds me; I must give them a likeness from a book. Sue didn't look at the Staffordshire like I did. Not her thing.'

'Uh.' I was losing his attention. The engine moved backwards, picked up a coal wagon, moved forwards again and then stopped. 'Bugger it,' he said conversationally.

'I must be off. Thanks, Charlie.'

'Always a pleasure, Tim. Any time.'

'I'll let myself out.'

He nodded absently. 'Cheers, mate.' Another engine twitched and he brightened. 'Got it,' he said, bending over the rails to adjust something. I ducked under the tables and got to the side door without catching my jacket under the trestles. Still quite supple, I am, you see. Without having to eat any bran.

CHAPTER 21

The King's Road blew dust at me and I practically closed my eyes as I tramped up past Old Church Street. Not far down to my right was the centre of much of Chelsea's fame: Cheyne walk, Carlyle's house, the lot.

'I didna enjoy yer visit,' I muttered to myself, thinking of the old misery. Poor ancient Scotsman; he had to suffer sitting to Whistler. Enough to tax the endurance of anyone, let alone Carlyle. Whistler was dreadful with his sitters and was always scraping off what he'd done to start afresh.

As I crossed the top end of Cadogan Walk I paused. The street ran straight down from the King's Road to the Embankment and I could see the end of the vista where, in the distance, heavy traffic lights flashed past the junction.

The evening was getting hazy, settling into one of those Whistlerian studies of softened outlines under night-time tones. To turn off the King's Road was irresistible. The Harwells' house was about half way down on the left, in the middle of the steep terrace-cliff. It was silent now, stone-windowed. No hint of the baroque interior, the work of a human bower-bird decorating its nest in gaudy attraction, could be gleaned from outside. The grey-brick London facing above the first flight of entrance steps and the bay windows merged into the general penumbra of the gloaming. Most people would be home by now, sitting down to eat, slumped in front of the telly. I'd spent longer with Charlie than I intended and here I was, roaming about indecisively back at the scene of the original crime. Sue would be waiting; I looked at my watch, still unwilling to break the inconsequential train of thought nagging the back of my mind.

It was nearly half past seven.

I sat down on the low wall bordering the front garden and the pavement to ponder. The street was quietly cluttered with parked cars, haif-lamplighted, it seemed, by the standards along its edge. Glowing windows in some uncurtained houses cast beams across the shrubs and asphalt under the darkening sky. If it were not for the bright lights and heavy traffic of the Embankment at the far end of the road I might have been in some older suburban enclave instead of a populated London borough.

A Mini turned into the street above me to my right after a pause at pavement crossing-point, where the driver must have glanced up and down to see the all clear. It picked up speed as it came nearer and then slowed, so that I automatically glanced up to see whether it would stop outside Harwell's. There were two people in the car and, as it reduced speed, the passenger on my side opened his window and moved his hand into it. The blessed uncurtained window-light across the road caught the gun barrel in a sharp tubular shine as he poked it out through the opening towards me. Without even thinking I tipped backwards into the front flower border behind the wall as the sharp double-bang rang out and his first shots missed me. The Mini squealed to a halt.

I remember thinking clearly, as I pressed myself into the dirty soil behind the wall, crushing a dejected shrub and the remains of some daisies beneath me, that he must have at least four more shots left, if not more. If he wasn't satisfied that my wild backward fling over the wall was the result of bullet-impact he'd get out and finish me off. Chances were, he'd get out and finish me off anyway if he really meant business. All I could do would be to run like hell and hope. Then I heard the car door open. Nobby had said that these were professionals; he was right.

A foot hit the ground. In about five seconds he'd put the rest of his bullets into my head if I just stayed where I was. My knee came up under me, shaking. It was a fat chance, almost useless: all I could hope was that he'd

162

not hit anything too vital as I ran, as his bullets ripped into the back of me. No, damn it, I thought suddenly, I'll charge him, the sod; that'll be better than getting it in the back like a fleeing rabbit.

Then the miracle happened.

The white Rover 3.5 with its luminous orange stripe must have careened round the same corner the Mini had just turned with its blue lights flashing and its 'Police' sign glaring blood-red. The noise of its siren, suddenly unleashed, hammered the street fit to split the eardrums, like a whooping destroyer doing a half-turn at full Action Stations. I heard a shout, two fast retreating steps and the scream of tyres preceding a slamming door as the Mini took off at full tilt with the police car right up its behind. It blasted off straight towards the Embankment as I emerged cautiously from the front garden to watch the two cars tearing off as though they were glued together in one of those mock-comic movies glorifying unending cops-and-robbers car chases during which a fortune's worth of equipment gets destroyed.

You can't do that sort of thing in London. Not for very far, anyway.

The police driver, correctly trained, had his brakes on well before the Mini's. I saw them flash bright scarlet, cross-reflected in parked cars and windows, at a well-judged distance before the end of the Street. The Rover practically stood on its nose. The Mini's brakes were much later, almost an afterthought, as its driver veered left with the idea of crossing the nearby traffic stream in a gap that would leave the policemen behind. It was a good risk, worth taking, but it didn't come *off*. There was a slam-thud, like a dustbin lid hitting the pavement, as a huge lorry collected the Mini on its front bumper before the driver had even thought about going for his brakes. As the combined mass slid out of sight with a metallic, spark-showered, scraping noise I saw the lorry's front end rear up almost absent-mindedly, like a St Bernard trying to mount a Sealyham, as it climbed over the Mini beneath it. By the time I had sprinted down the road and turned the corner into the Embankment to see where the momentum had slid them to, it was all over. One of the policemen had the lorry's nearside door open, shouting at the driver to come out before the petrol-reeking mess caught fire. The lorry, after its initial rearing, had settled its bulk quietly down to the road again. You could hardly see anything of the Mini squashed beneath it.

CHAPTER 22

Nobby Roberts drank some coffee from the plastic cup that Johnson had provided, glanced round at the lividly-lighted office in Chelsea police station, grimaced and looked narrowly at his colleague.

'Haven't you got anything better than this?'

Johnson gave him a look, sighed, tipped his chair back upright and reached to his lower desk drawer, the deep one.

He got out a half-empty bottle of supermarket whisky and three plastic cups. I've never known the CID to be very far from the hard stuff. Nobby gestured in my direction.

'He looks as though he could use it,' he said, with satisfaction. 'Face is still as white as a sheet.'

Johnson filled the three plastic cups each half-way up, pushed ours towards us and picked up his own. I took a heavy swallow and shivered. My second swallow finished the cup. Johnson refilled it without the slightest expression and then did the same to his own and Nobby's. The two of them watched me.

'Feeling better now?'

'Yes.'

There was something very comforting about the hardwood-furnished utilitarian office that Johnson obviously shared with an absent colleague. It was after nine o'clock but neither he nor Nobby had made the slightest remark about the time, as though it were quite normal for them to be working at thai hour. Papers littered Johnson's desk but he had a neat sort of look, like an organized man, always ready for inspection.

'Bit of luck for you,' he said smugly, for the fourth time that evening. 'Bright squad car man; Mini's number rang a bell and he radioed back for confirmation. Once they knew it was a nicked car he and the driver went after it. They tailed it from the King's Road until central came through on the blower. Then they let rip. Our boys love a chase but they don't like it to end like this one. Not usually, anyway, though I can't say I'm sorry this time.'

'I'd like to have their names,' I said, throat on whisky-fire. 'If you don't mind. For appreciation. They saved my life.'

'All contributions gratefully received,' said Johnson unemotionally. 'To all police charities, of course.' He grinned, caught a look from Nobby and straightened his face.

'None of that,' said Nobby absent-mindedly. 'Everyone's been taught a lesson, including Tim.'

I finished my second whisky and looked at him with a bit more sparkle. 'Look here,' I said, without heat, 'all I did was to walk down a street and sit down. To think. Nothing more than that. Could have been anyone.'

'Ha!' Nobby's voice was sharp. 'It wasn't me, Officer. Must be a mistake. Of course it was all to do with you! You were amateur sleuthing again; visiting the Scene of the Crime and all that crap. Well, I hope you've learnt something this time. If it hadn't been for our patrol car we'd be investigating your bullet-riddled body right now and I'd have to be asking Sue to avoid looking at your punctured ugly mug. What a dreadful thought.'

'Thank you very much.'

He grinned. He seemed to be quite stimulated. I began to be aware that Nobby liked real cases, real nastiness, as a proper challenge to his talents. So did Johnson. Neither of them was a time-serving type. You could irritate Nobby unendingly with misdemeanours but put a real crime under his nose and his tail would begin to wag like that of a terrier smelling rats. Both of them liked to be in the centre of things.

He picked up the notes they'd got from the Chelsea station computer.

'A real pair,' he murmured. 'Real bad lads. Not any more, though.'

I looked over his shoulder at the information again. The two men in the Mini, or what was left of them, had been extricated and identified with remarkable speed after the heavy breakdown crane had lifted the lorry clear. Not that it could have been very difficult; there was a decent quantity of information on record.

'Logan, James. Born Belfast, 1950. Service in the British Army. Service in Southern Africa as mercenary. Security adviser to demolition and waste materials recovery company, South London. Absent abroad on various occasions. Detained at Heathrow on request of Belgian police but released after questioning. Detained Amsterdam, 1982, and released again. Current status: unemployed.

'Stewart, William. Born Glasgow, 1948. Service in Scottish regiment. Settled Catford, South London, 1978. Jobs: driver, porter, assistant to antique dealer, car deliveries. Offences: car theft, grievous bodily harm, breaking and entering. Current status: mini-cab driver.'

The wheelman, obviously.

Their photographs stared woodenly at me. Nobby scratched his head. 'You've seen them before?'

'Yes.'

'They are the two that came to Harwell's house? You're absolutely sure?'

'Yes. It's them all right. I thought one—Logan it must have been—was a squaddie, an ex-army type.'

Johnson finished his paper cupful of whisky. 'Both are. Were. Someone wanted you killed. Thank God they're not on my manor any more.'

'They might have been looking for someone else.'

Johnson looked at Nobby and the two of them shook their heads. 'Very doubtful. That type don't waste themselves and they rarely make mistakes. It happens, of course, but I doubt it this time. And outside Harwell's house? Who else would they be after? They'd met you before.'

'Maybe someone else who's got into the race, like—like me.'

'With a broken nose and a heavy physique? I suppose it's possible.'

'Thanks.'

'One way or the other, Tim, someone's tried to kill you and I believe it was for a purpose. I think you were the target. They must have been watching that house since the murder.'

I felt indignant; the whole thing had become too personal. 'What I don't understand is why. I don't know anything more than anyone else but someone obviously thinks I do. It must be something I've done or said.'

Nobby picked up his notes. 'Let's go over it again. Apart from being at the Bank, you went to Morris Goldsworth's and then to Charlie Benson's. Nowhere else at all?'

'Nowhere.'

He scratched his chin. 'Morris Goldsworth I'll come to in a minute. He's more my end of town.' He cocked an eyebrow at Johnson. 'Charlie Benson? Your territory.'

Johnson shook his head. 'Charlie's well-known local trade. Hardly one of your big-time international hit-man hirers. He's not entirely clean, of course. They never are. He's too familiar by half with one or two of our uniformed branch.' He shrugged. 'So what? We all have to live here. I've no doubt that Charlie handles the odd dodgy piece, plunders the odd unknowing customer. It doesn't put him in the murderer bracket, now does it? He's a Chelsea boy; lived in Chelsea all his life, born and bred here. His dad was a butcher, put out of business by supermarkets. I agree that he'll handle anything but he's not big-time, not Charlie. Look at all that bloody awful china he sells. I mean, he does very little silver, which is always a bent dealer's trade, only a bit of jewellery through that girl in the shop, and a limited amount of flash gear like ormolu clocks and fancy Frenchy stuff. The rest is paintings and furniture, mainly furniture. Bloody awful a lot of it is, too. He knew the Harwells from way back. I don't see a local boy like Charlie doing in old Harwell. He's too fond of those toy trains of his to put himself at risk that way.'

Nobby held out his cup and Johnson obligingly poured the rest of his whisky out between the three of us. I made a mental note to make sure I returned his hospitality with interest. Whether Johnson's professional judgement was good or not, I decided that his heart was in the right place, which is all one asks of a policeman, really.

Nobby took a sip from his cup. 'Local boy or not, it doesn't put him out of the running. Everyone's a local boy somewhere, like the Krays.'

'Morris Goldsworth was a local boy,' I said. 'Charlie Benson reckons he started out from this area.'

Nobby sucked a tooth. 'He's very smooth now. Typical West End gallery stuff. High overheads, high risk, heavy investment, high margins. They've got to be, to pay off. His gallery has to have backing.'

'It has; Arabs, I believe. Or an Arab.'

'And a bank.'

'Eh?'

'He has more than one backer. He got money from more than one source.'

'How do you know?'

'I'm in the Fraud Squad, remember? We once did an analysis, on a college course, of the sources of capital of the London art market for a case study. It was good fun. We never got anywhere near the real figure, of course, but part of the realistic aspect of it was that we got the shareholdings of all the main galleries and auctioneers as an exercise in digging up facts and figures from Companies House and other sources. I knew I was going to be on the art side so I kept the stuff in my folder. It's very difficult, because of nominee shareholdings, but I've got a lot of that kind of information. Morris Goldsworth's

169

gallery is financed from Bahrain and an overseas bank registered in the Bahamas. Typical stuff.'

'I don't suppose there'll be any connection between him and those two in the Mini?'

'I doubt it. We'll try, of course. And we do know, on the QT through your friend Charles, that he's after a Whistler. Although we don't have any direct evidence of connection with Harwell.'

'Except that Goldsworth is or was from Chelsea. Charlie says that he used to be a runner for Harwell's business.'

'Except that. Which I shall talk to him about tomorrow. And, of course, we'll check on the last moments of our two dead hit-men. Goldsworth will probably close like a clam. They usually do. My guess is that he'll say that he's acting for himself. That no "client" exists. That's what usually happens.' He shook himself slightly, as though in reproach for an over-confidence as he looked at me objectively. 'Now for Christ's sake will you go home and stop playing at detectives, there's a good boy? I don't think you're in danger right now because it'll take them time to replace Logan and Stewart. Unless of course—' he smiled a bland, sarcastic smile—'you think we're dealing with a combination of the Black Hand and Al Capone? We'll keep an eye on you, of course, but I hope you won't mind if we don't ask the SAS to protect you just yet?'

I got up with dignity. There's simply no dealing with Nobby when he's in one of his flippant moods.

'You can give me a lift home,' I said. 'Unless, that is, you've got doubts about driving after an intake of three large doubles?'

His face didn't move. Johnson smiled secretively as he pressed a button on his telephone console and spoke.

'Tell transport to take Mr Simpson home, would you, George? We'll be working on here for a while.'

CHAPTER 23

I woke up a bit late. She was showered and dressed ready to go to the Tate. She put a cup of tea down on the bedside table beside me and scowled down at my face. She is very pretty and I wanted to hold her but I looked up obediently.

'Have you told me everything?

'Everything.'

'Are you sure?'

'Certain, miss.'

Her scowl deepened. 'I don't believe you. You're holding something back.'

'Christ! How much more do you want? Goldsworth's, Charlie's, being shot at, hours down the nick?' I struggled upright and picked up the tea. 'Hey? What else do I have to do? Fly an aeroplane?'

She pursed her lips. 'Why did they shoot at you? What possible good would it do? You haven't found the Whistler, have you?'

'Of course not!'

'There isn't—now be honest with me, Tim—there isn't some sort of Other Woman involved, is there?'

'Oh my God! Between you and Nobby I may as well join the Salvation Army! I suppose you've been mulling over everything all night?'

'I have. I've never come across anything like it. It doesn't make sense. Have you been telling me the truth? About everything?'

'For God's sake.' I sipped the tea in resignation. 'Ask Nobby, if you like. You and he and the Band of Hope.'

'Oh, Nobby! You'd tell him anything! Why didn't you collect me to come with you?'

'There wasn't time.'

'Of course there was time!'

'All right. All right. I just didn't think of it. I didn't take you into my plans. Not just for those two visits. And thank heaven I didn't. You might have been shot outside

171

Harwell's.'

'Rubbish!' She didn't sound quite so certain this time, though.

'Look,' I said. 'You'll be late for work. Why don't you just nip along to the Tate and keep busy, eh? If anything more happens I'll phone you. It's all in the hands of Nobby and his minions. I have to go to the Bank; Jeremy won't exactly be pleased.'

'Jeremy'll have a blue fit!' Through her frown and vehemently her lip suddenly quivered. 'It's not very nice of you just to try and get rid of me, Tim. You agreed to my being part of all this. Your partner. I—I'm frightened. When you didn't come home last night I imagined all sorts of terrible things. You don't know what I thought.'

She made me feel dreadful.

I reached out to take her hand. 'Sue, sweetheart, don't be upset. I've told you everything that happened. Everything. I'm sorry. I suppose that when the going starts to get dangerous my natural reaction is to clear the decks. Nobby would kill me if anything happened to you; he's appointed himself a sort of Dutch Uncle to you. I've been so used to working solo that I didn't think. I promise to bring you in on anything more that happens. All right?'

'All right.' Her tone was mollified. She gave me another sideways look. 'You're going to the Bank? Nowhere else?'

'Cross my heart. To the Bank.'

She went and collected her coat. She raised a finger at me. 'I want to know! If anything happens, I want to know!'

'Yes, miss.'

She put her tongue out and left. I collected myself together, finished the tea, showered, dressed, and made some toast and fresh tea. I was sitting in the morning sunlight, eating the toast and reading the *Financial Times* when the phone rang. With a sigh, I went across to the receiver and picked it up. Work or trouble, I thought, bracing myself. It was neither: Charles Massenaux spoke.

'Tim?'

'Oh hullo, Charles. How are you? This is a rare pleasure. So early in the morning.'

'Tim, I've got to see you.'

'Really? Well, sure, but—'

'No buts. It's urgent.'

'You mean now?'

'Now.'

I was taken aback. Men like Charles depend on an atmosphere of unhurried expertise to gain their living; fluster is anathema to the fine art auctioneer. 'Charles, look here, things have been a bit dicey at present. I have to clear some matters up at the Bank. Is it really that urgent?'

'Tim, I need to see you *now.* I can't talk on the phone. I'm afraid I've overdone things. Look, I know you've helped me but I've helped you too. A lot. This time it may be too much: my head's on the chopping-block. It'll be me for the Eastern Front at best if you can't help. Can you come?'

'The Eastern Front? Christ! Stay put, dear boy: I'm on my way.'

'Not here. I can't be seen talking to you here.'

'Bloody hell. Surely things can't be as bad as that?'

There was an exasperated silence. I made up my mind very rapidly. 'Go to the corner of Bond Street and Piccadilly. I'll come by in the Jaguar and pick you up. We'll talk in it on the way to the Bank, then take it from there. OK?'

'Done. See you on Piccadilly.' His voice was relieved.

'Right.'

Normally I'd have tubed from South Ken but as it happened there was a slot I could park in behind the Bank, temporarily anyway. It turned out to be a blessed decision; I was going to need the car that day. I left the cheerful morning-room, the toast, the tea, and shot out like a Le Mans-style starter. A bit of congestion at Knightsbridge and then there he was, hopping about on the pavement on the corner of Bond Street. He leapt in as I stopped for him and started talking to me as though he'd been given a shot of cocaine. As we threaded our way eastwards I managed to get a question in here and there until, by the time we'd reached the City, he'd calmed down and ordered his thoughts quite a bit. I parked the car and took him straight upstairs.

'This couldn't have worked out better,' I said, as I led him through Jeremy's ante-room and into the office, where Jeremy roosted behind his desk, dictating pompously to Clara. He looked up as we burst in, his face congested. I held up a restraining hand and spoke soothingly.

'Sorry about the rush, Jeremy, but could you clear the decks? Charles has something important to tell you. It has to do with our current discussions.'

CHAPTER 24

I pulled the Jaguar up outside the Tate Gallery and looked at my watch. Just gone three. An eventful, no, a momentous morning and a working lunch-time gone. Well, I thought, she wants to be in on things. Strike while the iron's hot, while you're feeling decisive. I went up the stairs two at a time, through the marble hallways, down into the basement, along a corridor, into the administrative area. She was standing with her back to me talking to a grey-haired man in a dark suit, a senior sort of fellow. They were looking at a type of Rossetti someone had parked on a table against the wall. As I came up behind them they turned to look at me. Sue's face lit up with surprise. I peered at the painting. It depicted a rather blurry, watery sort of female with gingery hair like Nobby's who was dressed in a flowing robe that usefully relieved the artist from having to demonstrate too much anatomical accuracy. She was peering at a mirror and there was some foliage about the place. I shook my head.

'That's not really a Rossetti, is it?' I queried.

The elderly man cocked his head to one side and looked at me.

'No?' It was a slight challenge.

'Rosa Corder, I'd say.'

'Eh?'

'Rosa Corder. Mistress to Charles Augustus Howell. Painted by Whistler, she was. And the rest.'

'I am aware,' he began drily, 'that—'

'She painted Rossettis. For Howell. And Fuselis.'

His face betrayed agitation. 'You're confusing me, Mr— er—?'

'Simpson. Sorry. Rosa Corder used to paint "Fuselis" and "Rossettis" for Charles Augustus Howell who was an entrepreneur. And a crook. Howell knew what would sell and what he could handle. He was a Chelsea type. The supply of real Rossettis was a bit difficult so he got his

175

Rosa to supplement it. There used to be quite a few dud Rossettis about. I'd say that was one of them.'

He smiled then. 'I must agree that it is not authentic. How interesting your theory is. Actually I know about Rosa Corder.'

'Yes. Well. Sorry to interrupt.' I turned to Sue. 'Can you spare me a bit of time? Things are coming to a head.'

She goggled at me. I took her arm and steered her away from the grey man.

'Get your handbag,' I said. 'I need you now.'

'Tim,' she whispered urgently, 'that's one of the Directors! I—'

'Now. I promised you this morning. D'you want to come or not?'

She pulled back to look at me. 'This isn't some spoof idea of yours, is it? I mean, you're not thinking of taking me back to the flat and—you know—'

'No, I'm not!'

She nipped back into a little office, came out, murmured a few words to the grey man, picked up a handbag and followed me obediently upstairs. I trotted her out to the car, tucked her in, and set off.

'We're going to the Hilton,' I said, as we whizzed across the King's Road and turned towards Knightsbridge.

'Why?'

'Because I want to talk to Mr Andy Casey of Chicago. He has a lot of explaining to do. Particularly about advertisements.'

'He has? Him?' Her face suddenly puckered. 'You don't mean—'

'Yes, I do. According to what Nobby says, anyway.'

We shot alongside the Hilton and left the car under the nose of a doorman. Reception said that Mr Casey wasn't in. I glared at the head porter. Sue smiled sweetly and asked if Mr Casey had said where he might be. The head porter melted a little and said that one of his porters had been talking to Mr Casey about trains. He ambled off and came back with a livened old codger.

''Sright,' he said. 'Charing Crawse.' I looked it up for him.

'Eh?'

'To Charing Cross. Mr Casey. The three-forty-five he went for. Few minutes ago.'

I glanced at the reception hall clock. It was three-thirty.

'Where to?' I demanded, but I knew the answer before he even said it.

'Hastings line. For—'

'St Leonards, Warrior Square,' I chorused with him as I ran Sue out to the car, thanking my stars that I'd been using it instead of Underground trains all that day.

CHAPTER 25

It takes the train about an hour and three-quarters to get to Hastings. I must have done it in nearly the same time. The train has to stop quite a lot once it gets past Tonbridge and I didn't, but then the train doesn't have to worry about lorries full of gypsum that can only do five miles an hour uphill, and idiots in vans delivering farm produce to village groceries. I pulled into Norman Road just about the time she should have been shutting up shop. For some reason Sue insisted on coming in with me, as though I might have had time to daily. I called out as we buzzed in through the door but the dyed-blonde lady didn't come out from behind the bead curtain covering the alcove which contained her little office, her cosy fire and the plump chaise-longue which Sue said she would have employed in my seduction.

She was dead.

'Shotgun!' I practically shouted as I grabbed Sue and tried to hide her eyes from the dreadful stare, the gaping wound with its great red stains and the sprawled ungainly limbs revealed in their cold unattractive flesh. I thought Sue's nails would go right through my arm as she hooked them into me like hydraulic claws, her eyes tight shut. She didn't say a single word. She just clung tight, so tight that, after what I thought was a decent interval, I had trouble disengaging her. We didn't have much time.

I took a look around the homely shop with its bright white china and its bulging Staffordshire dogs. Yet another Prince Albert stared back at me, intact. Leaving Sue where she stood with me in the bead-curtained doorway I stepped carefully into the little alcove-office where the body of the dyed lady lay on the lino floor. The desk looked undisturbed. A few cushions were strewn on the chaise-longue and the prints and papers on the walls looked ruffled. The single-bar electric fire was out. Bending down carefully, I looked into the well below the pedestal desk where dust and grit had accumulated from her long hours of patient sitting. A white card gleamed at me from the darkness.

It was mine. The one I had given her with instructions to call me. I picked it up carefully and turned it over. Scrawled on the back in black ballpoint was the simple legend: Howell, 15 Carradine Road.

'This is it,' I said quickly to Sue, steering her back to the door. 'Call the police. I'll go on ahead.'

'No!'

'Sue, for heaven's sake! This is serious! I'm going to find 15 Carradine Road. There's no time to lose.'

'No!' Her voice was fierce, even angry. 'Either we both go to the police or we both go to the road. I'm not staying here. And I'm not leaving you.'

'The police will take time. They'll have to know that he's armed. They have procedures.'

'I know! Come on! That poor old man! It'll be just like his brother! Don't just stand there!'

So that was it: there was nothing more I could do. Marvelling at her control and her courage, I rushed her out to the car again. I could guess at the area in which we'd find Carradine Road because the dyed lady had indicated it; the lost limbo-land of great half-Italianate terraces to the north of us, around the churches, above the grottoed valley of Septimus Burton's original layout. Twisting the wheel, I heeled the car right at the top of Norman Road and tacked my way through the tiny bends that shield the upper, wider reaches of road. I had to squint at the street names as we rolled upwards among the high façades of divided houses, all with their rows of parked cars in the gutters, like a North London suburb. Carradine Road was a cross-street up to the left away from the main thoroughfare and the lights. No. 15 was at the end of a terrace, a high rearing wall of dark bay windows, arched attics and rusted downpipes. It looked derelict.

I pulled the car into the gutter and sat looking at the house, two or three doors away from us, for a moment.

'Come on!' Sue was impatient.

'Stay here! No, better still, find a telephone.'

Without saying a word she got out. I had to nip round the car very smartly and grab her.

'All right!' I hissed. 'Take it easy. We'll go in quietly.'

She gave me another ferocious look. I grinned at her. '"Quem não tem cão, caca con gato,"' I said softly.

'What? What's that?'

'It's an old Brazilian saying. Or it may have been Portuguese. It means "he who has no dog hunts with a cat."'

Her reply was unprintable. Absolutely unprintable. Nice girls simply do not use language like that.

The bulk of No. 15 loomed above us. Dark bay windows at lower levels gave way to flat arched upper sashes. The building had been sandstone-yellow once: now it was blackened, streaked, unkempt. The front garden was untended, dirty, scrap-strewn. Yet the architecture was handsome, almost grandiose. The roof ended in broad eaves that jutted out in a wide flat moulding dentillated by support-blocks of bracketed shapes. It reminded me again of Osborne and the Isle of Wight. The front door looked unused and uninviting, without the usual row of flat-doorbells that studded the side-panels on other houses. This great dark building was still all of a piece, undivided. Its front doorway was a double effort above wide steps: there would be a decently generous hallway behind it. I beckoned to Sue.

'Let's try the basement,' I said.

We trod carefully round the side of the front staircase and down a brief flight beside it to the basement-well. The basement door was set directly below the main front one. It was a dirty black affair with two old reeded glass panels thick with dust, but it opened at the turn of its knob. A dark passage receded from it. I led Sue straight into the gloom as quickly as I dared, heading forward until my foot hit the first step of the stairway up to the main floor. Fortunately it was covered with a grimed threadbare carpet that muffled any noise as we creaked gently upwards. At the top the stairs did a right turn to emerge below the main staircase of the house, into the hall. I stood in the stair-doorway for a moment to get used to the light.

The hallway itself was in half-darkness but from upstairs somewhere a faint yellow glow aided the light from the glazing around the front doors. I heard a voice high above. Stepping carefully, I moved into the hallway, my leather soles grating very slightly on the chequered marble floor. Sue was dead quiet; her shoes must have been rubber-soled. The main floor was still; behind us, presumably, were back rooms above the basement kitchen. I moved to the bottom of the main staircase; it was a fine one even though dilapidated. The smell of damp and dust was accentuated by the wallpaper and some glazed lincrusta cladding which were both beginning to come loose in places. Plaster mouldings at ceiling level were missing odd bits. This was definitely a neglected house, lacking maintenance, but it had not been so for long. My guess was that it had just started, perhaps an odd few years ago, to miss the spending its upkeep demanded.

The voice was heard again, louder, I guessed in an upper bedroom. Gesturing to Sue, I crept up to the wide first-floor landing. The rooms here would still be generous, high- ceilinged and spacious but all the doors were closed. At the cross-end of the landing a half-staircase went up at right-angles then turned, a right-angle again, to go straight up from my vision to the next floor. It was steeper than a modern staircase, presumably set across the wide landing to save space for rooms. I thought it an odd arrangement as I reached it but the interiors of nineteenth-century houses contain every quirk of arrangement you can think of. Sue practically urged me up it as the voice was replied to by someone else; she was right behind me as we reached the top.

The light came from a room set a few feet down the landing from the top of this staircase. Up here the proportions were lower, narrower, less generous. Up here would sleep the children, lesser members of the family, perhaps there would have been a nursery. One flight more would take you to servants' rooms, attics. There would be a back staircase somewhere.

I crept along the landing to the door and squinted in around the jamb. At the far side of the room facing me was an old man I recognized as a Harwell. Next to him, stock still, was Andy Casey. Beside them, on the floor, propped against the skirting, were two paintings. One was the view of the London reach full of shipping with the figures in the foreground exactly as in the instamatic snap I'd seen. Jo Hiffernan, I thought, and that is probably Legros after all. Whistler brought him to England and then they fell out over Whistler's treatment of Jo when he got back from Valparaiso. Whistler even struck Legros.

I shook myself slightly. It was no time for biographical musing. The other painting was the full length portrait of Maud Franklin, hand on hip, carrying a muff. Her pale face was narrow and she gave the impression of being slender. Another victim of Whistler's, but hers was a happier ending; she married a rich Parisian and lived on the Champs Elysées. On the floor beside her portrait were three or four large sheets of paper, placed carefully on the boards of a folio cover. Christ, I thought, those must be etchings; this hoard, in this dark gloomy house, is a minor treasure trove.

Facing the two men, with his back to me, was the great bulk of Charlie Benson, twenty-odd stone of it. Under his right arm, pointing straight at them, was a double-barrelled sawn-off shotgun. The shock of seeing him was worse than the shock of recognizing his voice when I saw his head move from the back; there was no doubt who it was.

'Mine,' he said, in a voice low with threat. 'They are mine. My family's.'

'No.' Old Leonard Harwell's voice was fearful but firm. 'My father bought them fair and square. Fifty years ago. We've still got the receipts.'

'You.' Charlie's voice increased its threatening tone. Contempt and hatred were conveyed with his words. 'You lot. Called yourself Harwells. You and your stupid house, like a Christmas cake. You're from Howell's brats: the whole world knows that. Bastards from one of his fancy women. That bloody cheat. Swindling bloody swine, he was. Cheated Whistler out of his paintings and cheated us out of ours. You did. Your dad did.'

'It's not true! He bought them fair and square. From a dealer in the King's Road. Let me show you—'

'Stay where you are!' The shotgun flicked upward as his body tensed. 'Don't move! Don't spin yarns to me! I bloody *know*, see? Those paintings belonged to my family. Whistler gave them to us. My great-grandmother was one of his models!'

'Mistresses you mean.' The old man's voice was tremulous but he kept his head straight. 'You think you're descended from him, don't you? That her child was Whistler's. That he gave these paintings to make up for it when he had no money? Well, it's not true; the one maybe, but the other—'

'Shut up! Shut up! These paintings belong to my family. Howell cheated us out of them. That's how you got them. Don't give me that King's Road dealer story! They're mine! Do you hear me? Mine! I've been looking for those for years.'

Andy Casey spoke. God knows what he must have been thinking. In the circumstances he was being pretty brave, to put it mildly. 'Look,' he began, reasonably, 'can't we just calm down and work this out? There's no need to—'

'Shut up!' Benson's voice moved towards hysteria. 'You! You fucking Yank! I hate you! You think you can barge in here with your bloody money and steal those paintings! Well, I'll show you what we do with carpetbaggers like you! Got here in the nick of time, didn't I? Eh? Here, see how you like—you—'

The clench of his hands stiffened. His massive fingers closed. I leapt round the door and performed one of the worst line-out fouls I've ever perpetrated on anyone from behind. I drove my knee into the back of his, clamped my left arm round his neck and jerked him backwards with my right arm holding his gun hand, to pull it upwards. The explosion was terrific because both barrels went off simultaneously but by that time they were pointing upwards at the ceiling. The effect was devastating. It seemed to bring the whole roof down.

Great chunks of plaster and moulding cascaded on to us. A cloud of white dust obliterated my vision as I staggered backwards through the door, attempting to make the best of my surprise attack on a man much more powerful than me. I was holding Charlie tightly round the neck, trying to pull him over but he wouldn't come; he stopped and drove his elbow back into my stomach. Caught leaning backwards, hands full, the blow hit me like a pile-driver. I doubled up and sat down in the centre of the landing, leaving Charlie standing there with the shotgun still in his hand. Sue, at the stairhead, screamed. Then the worst possible thing happened.

'Tim?' Andy Casey came shakily out through the billowing dust. 'Tim Simpson? Is that you?'

He obviously couldn't see properly. Charlie Benson turned. I knew what he would do next. Horror moved my legs. As he swung the brutal, heavy shotgun in an arc, so as to get in a blow that would smash Casey's skull, I tackled him low, just above the knees, as hard as I could. Rugby forwards often have to move off the ground they have been brought down on, so it wasn't entirely an inexperienced assault. The problem was lack of space. The shotgun-swing missed and Charlie went backwards across the landing with me driving him. Sue let out a terrific shriek and leapt out of the way at the stairhead. Our combined bulk missed her as it went into the one gap available: the staircase.

I remember thinking, as we went over, that this must be what shooting Niagara must feel like. Charlie went first and, because of my grip, I went right over on top of him, swinging up what seemed high in the air, poised above the dreadfully steep fall for a somersault. I remember thinking as well that I must hold on to him because if I let go and he got free at any point, he'd kill me, sure as fate. So I held tight; held tight as we crashed over and over down the first half-flight of stairs made entirely of hard sharp corners that bashed my head, rabbit-punched my kidneys, cracked my cartilages. At the bottom our combined mass hit the slender wooden balusters and we smashed straight through the right-angle, going plumb over the vertical drop to the main landing below.

I nearly lost Charlie then; the impact at the smashed railing knocked all the wind out of me and my clenched fists slackened. I just caught his leg near the ankle with one hand as we sailed into the void. It helped to turn him under me as he went first, head down, great bulk above the black beard, me on top of that. The impact was terrific when the thirty-five stone of us hit the landing: a great crump! of bodies and a snapping and splintering. It knocked me senseless for several seconds. A split baluster-splinter several inches long had driven its sharp spiked end into my leg so that, when I tried to move, a stab of agony shot up my thigh. I was panic-stricken. Charlie, I thought, he'll kill me. My ears sang. I turned on my side and pulled the big wooden spike out, trying to roll away, duck a blow.

He didn't move. I got upright and heaved myself on to one knee to look at him. His head was over one way and

I'd seen that before; his neck was broken. Cautiously, I moved to go towards him.

'Tim!' Sue flung herself round my neck, knocking me off balance again. I got one hand on to a nearby wall and managed to brace myself while she hung on to me, staggering slightly at the load. Charlie was dead. The great bulk didn't move, the neck angle was awful. It was like looking at a dead bull. Indirectly, I'd killed him by landing on top; my ankle-grab did that.

'Are you all right? Are you all right?' she kept babbling at me over and over again. I made a few placatory noises and tried to give a reassuring pat but it was difficult with her hanging on like that. Gratifying, mark you, but difficult.

An ashen figure came down to the smashed stair-turn. It stood above us, peering over into the gap. The ceiling-plaster may have been the main reason why the hair and face were chalky-white, not to mention the floury-looking clothes, but somehow I knew that Andy Casey was not looking his normal healthy self under all that dust. He gaped at the motionless bulky body below, then at me.

'Great tackle, champ,' he said hoarsely, his voice full of awe. 'What my old coach would have called the Ultimate Stopper.'

I managed to brace myself upright for a few more seconds. Suddenly I didn't feel at all well. 'I think I owe you an apology,' I said. Then I slid down the wall. I couldn't hold up with Sue round me any longer, because she was just too heavy for me like that. It's not often the case, you know; I don't usually find her heavy at all.

CHAPTER 26

There were four of us for breakfast at the Hilton: Andy Casey, Sue, myself and Charles Massenaux. I used to be suspicious of the American business breakfast but, as with many transatlantic institutions, I have come to like it. You get something done before the day's routine starts clamping down, there's no alcohol, and you can righteously eat a decent plate of bacon and eggs which you wouldn't normally cook without feeling guilty. Since Andy Casey was leaving for Chicago at noon, it was doubly convenient.

'You'll have plenty of time before your flight,' I told him. 'Sue will go with you to Harrods to advise on your family gift shopping and you can go straight on to Heathrow from there.'

'Great.' The clear blue eyes were appreciative. The freckled skin glowed with health again. He turned to Sue. 'It really is very kind of you. I'm hopeless at buying things for my wife and kids.'

'It'll be a pleasure.' Sue meant it. 'I'm looking forward to spending all that money without feeling guilty myself.'

We all laughed then and it obviously broke the ice enough for Casey to broach the subject we hadn't dealt with yet.

'I really feel bad about my advertisements,' he said. 'I had no idea—really I didn't—that you were specifically trying to buy a Whistler. I got the agency to put them in the papers ahead of my arrival and during it, so that I could follow up the replies. Of course, I kept quiet about it because I didn't want any competition. I figured that you guys would get ahead of me, being locals, if you knew. I've always admired your Art Fund. That's why I didn't commission a dealer to find a Whistler either. I was going to use an expert to vet any painting that came up for a fee. I figured that way I'd get my Whistlers without having to pay a big margin to a gallery or having to bid against Freer or Getty or you or whoever at auction.'

'I thought it was Morris Goldsworth,' I said. 'Actually, it turns out, from what Nobby's told me, that Charlie Benson told Goldsworth he had a client for a Whistler and he'd do a deal with him if he could find one or get one at auction. He used the Winans name as a red herring, knowing all that story from his railway history. He must have nearly had heart failure when I told him that Morris was advertising for a Whistler. He'd agreed with Morris that they'd do it on the quiet to avoid stirring up too much trade interest. He hoped Morris would use his network of contacts to see if the Harwells were trying to sell the paintings at auction or into the trade. He had a strong notion that they existed but he wasn't sure and the Harwells were so close to home. Eventually his temper and impatience got the better of him. He knew Stewart as a heavy involved in the trade so he hired him and Logan to bully old George Harwell in Cadogan Walk. I intervened, by accident, but Benson returned with the two of them to carry on. That's what killed George Harwell. They found some of the Staffordshire in Charlie's place, hidden away, including the gardener I mentioned. He hadn't been able to resist it.'

Charles Massenaux finished his scrambled egg and took a sip of his coffee before asking, 'Was he really descended from Whistler?'

I shrugged slightly. 'It's possible. If you believe in heredity you could say that a love of railways combined with art and antiques plus a hot temper could be strong indicators.' I caught a quizzical look from him and smiled. 'I know; lots of people love railways, paintings and antiques and are bad-tempered. It's just a thought. Whistler liked porcelain, too.'

'The Harwells—they really are Fitz-Howells or whatever?'

'There seems little doubt of that. Leonard Harwell says he can find all sorts of family evidence. He was terrified, poor old bugger. The Harwells were chronically secretive and kept him hidden away in St Leonards, where they bought that house years ago. It has all sorts of goodies in it; the savings of years of antique dealing.'

'Why on earth didn't he go to the police?'

'When he heard of his brother's murder he was distraught. It seems he had a fair inkling of who was behind it. You know, Charlie Benson was well in with the local uniformed branch; Johnson admitted that. The Harwells were very suspicious of police involvement because they thought that they couldn't be trusted. The ad in the papers—he saw it in the *Trade* Gazette, by the way—came to him as a last chance. He thought that if he could sell the Whistlers he would get rid of the source of the violence; if he didn't have them any more he wouldn't be at risk.' I turned to Andy Casey. 'He didn't give his address? He arranged to meet you somewhere? So that he could check your bona fides first?'

'At the station. St Leonards station.' He shivered. 'We went back to this dark, ruinous old house. Then all the way upstairs. It gave me the creeps. I never had an experience anything like it. When the black-bearded guy with a shotgun burst in I nearly died of heart failure. I just couldn't believe it.'

'He moved very quickly once his two heavies were killed in the car. I suppose he thought someone might connect him with them. Questions would be asked. He probably could field them but he'd have little chance of pursuing the Harwells' Whistlers once that happened. He knew about the shop in Norman Road from the time the Granada followed me. Once he'd got the address from the woman he couldn't afford to leave her to tell me.'

Sue frowned down at her plate. Charles Massenaux shook his head. 'The—the fifty-pence piece and—and that. What was that all about?'

'Charlie had a way of working himself up into a filthy temper. He'd got a sort of mad hatred of Charles Augustus Howell burning in him. Somehow he believed that Whistler, and hence he, had been massively cheated. Howell did cheat Whistler, of course; Charlie must have known how Howell died from local Chelsea gossip. He re-enacted the scene on old Harwell after he was dead.'

'Jesus Christ.'

'Yes. Well. We are having breakfast so I won't go on any further. Except to say that when George Harwell said to us that "they say they're from his family" I think he had a pretty good notion who was behind the two hard men. He may have thought that going to the police would only infuriate Charlie Benson further. What worried me was how it was that Charlie chose his moment to push for the Whistlers just about the same time that Harwell wrote to me with the intention of getting rid of them. Leonard thinks that whoever sold Charlie the Walter Greaves tipped him off. That Walter Greaves had been in Chelsea for donkey's years. If it was an old local who Charlie chatted up it's quite possible he may have recalled the Harwells' Whistlers. That would have set Charlie off. It was a family legend that the Bensons should have owned works by Whistler.' I looked at Sue. 'All the research we did into the legitimate side of the family was wasted. It was an old feud from the other side of the blanket, after all.'

Andy Casey pricked up his ears. 'Research? You researched into Whistler's family?'

'Yes. I'm afraid I—um—we thought the trouble might have been from his legitimate descendants who would mainly be Americans. Sue dug up some very interesting connections.'

'Could I—would you mind—could I have that information? Just for interest, in view of our, er, arrangements?'

'Of course. You are still quite happy about the arrangements, I hope?'

'Perfectly: I think it's ideal. In fact, I think you've been great about it. It is absolutely right that you have the Wapping scene for your Fund; you're a London merchant bank and you've been involved in merchant trade on the Thames since the nineteenth century. I'm delighted with the lady—' he gave Sue a gallant half-bow—'and the etchings. I almost feel we've taken too much.'

'Well, you got there first. It was your ads that did it. Old Leonard being too scared to contact us after what happened. And I imagine your clients in Albany and Baltimore will be very chuffed with the etchings due to the Whistler connection?'

'Right. They certainly will. And my board are overwhelmed at getting an original painting by the grandson of Chicago's founder.' He grinned. 'I'm not sure if I'll tell them that she was Whistler's English mistress. I'll have to think about that.' He cocked an eyebrow at Charles. 'You've no doubt that they're all genuine? We've paid the old Harwell guy well for them.'

'Oh, none. No doubt. Could tell they were Whistler's a mile off.' Charles turned to me. 'Nobby says that Morris Goldsworth isn't implicated at all?'

'Apparently not. Charlie used him as a feeler without telling him anything about the Harwells. I'm afraid I owe him an apology too. I must say I had mixed feelings when I saw the Walter Greaves in Charlie's shop. Apparently he really did buy it locally, though, through his own contacts.'

'That's a relief. Morris still doesn't know that I—you know—mentioned to you—'

'No. He doesn't.' I turned back to Andy Casey. 'That brings me on to my next subject.'

'Ah.' He held up a hand to stop me. 'I think you should know that I recommended that we collaborate with White's on this Brazilian deal before the events in St

Leonards. I forgot to mention that to you and Jeremy yesterday.'

I shook my head. 'It isn't that. Though thank you all the same. I think that *you* should know that we have just succeeded in acquiring—it was signed yesterday afternoon—a block of shares amounting to over thirty per cent of the stock of Christerby's. It was Charles here who alerted us to the availability of them. There were people in Certain Quarters who preferred to see the ownership stay British— it's a controlling interest, you see, and the staff themselves, that is, most of the senior staff led by Charles, were particularly keen on it. So who better than White's, with the celebrated Fund, to take over? Actually, Jeremy and I have been keen for some time to get into the wholesale side—if Charles will pardon the expression—and we have strong feelings about the expansion of the Art Fund into the States. A stake in Christerby's, which has been struggling to establish itself over there, has some interesting possibilities, because we have some ideas about the future development of the business.'

'Well I'll be damned! You Limeys really can get up off your asses when you want to.'

'Er, yes. Well. If our plans go ahead as we hope we'll need to raise money in the States and have a sort of tie-in, a local presence. You said you were impressed by our Art Fund, I recall, and you're obviously going to invest in art again. Jeremy and I wondered if you would be interested in one or two little schemes we have in mind? You've made a powerful hit with Jeremy and now you've met Charles, who'll be on the main board of Christerby's, and of course you know me. So what do you say?'

He put his coffee cup down carefully as he smiled. 'You mean you don't mind getting together with a Chicago Irish-American?'

'Ah—oh—well, I never thought of you that way, really. Just as a sort of Reliable Chap, you know. And in view of your interest in art . . .'

He held out his hand. 'It's a deal. Just tell me when you're ready.'

I took the firm grasp. 'Great. Come to think of it, if you're getting into this field and you want a symbol of Anglo-American cooperation, or Celtic-Anglo-Saxon cooperation if you prefer it, you couldn't do better than to start with a Whistler really, could you? There's no need to pull a face like that, Charles. I was speaking symbolically; the contentious aspects are over and done with now, you know.'

CHAPTER 27

Later that day, Jeremy and I had a memorable lunch. Coming on top of an ample breakfast at the Hilton, it left an afterglow of utterly satisfactory repletion. I let myself into the flat with a feeling that I deserved a certain contentment at the way things had gone. Sue was sitting on the big settee in front of the fireplace, under the marine painting by Clarkson Stanfield.

'How was the shopping?'

'Marvellous.' She gave me a significant look. 'He's very generous. Very generous. His wife has got one or two fabulous presents to come when he gets back. It was a revelation.'

'Good,' I said heartily, avoiding the narrowing eyes and meaning smile that hinted a million hints. 'I'm glad it went well. Bet he was glad to have your help.'

'He was.'

'Didn't offer you a pair of nylons or a stick of chewing gum for your cooperation, did—'

'Tim! Really! No, he didn't! He gave me a box of superb handmade chocolates and said he was looking forward to seeing me in Chicago when you come over. Apparently he thinks you'll be coming over often. With me.'

'Oh. Well. That's nice. Where are the chocolates?'

'I've eaten them.'

'All of them?'

'It wasn't a very big box. Quite small. But very expensive. Delicious. I thought I deserved them. Did you have a nice day at the office?'

'Er, not bad. Things are going quite well. Jeremy and I discussed some changes.'

'What changes?'

'Oh nothing. Just some business changes.'

Her teeth set in a line. 'What changes?'

'Business changes. Big boys' things.' I gave her a leering grin. 'Nothing for you to worry your pretty little head about.'

She missed me with the paperback she'd been reading and I dodged the lipstick case quite easily but she was dead accurate with the apple from the fruit-bowl on the coffee table. It caught me plumb centre on the nose and stung tears to my eyes as I closed on her, so that I couldn't see her face clearly as I grappled with her. Eventually I got her arms pinned to her sides and tumbled her back on to the settee, where the struggle continued with diminishing resistance until it ceased altogether and reversed, with interest.

Which was all very satisfactory, of course, but I couldn't help the thought nagging, afterwards, as she held me, that I never did find out where Sir Kensington Whistler got to. Without him, the whole thing might not have happened.

John Malcolm is the author of fifteen Tim Simpson mysteries, as well as a number of books on art and antiques. He was Chairman of the Crime Writers Association for 1994-5. He was also Chairman of the Trustees of Rye Art Gallery from 1995 to 2004.

He read engineering at Cambridge and then worked as an international marketing consultant, travelling extensively. He and his wife Geraldine, a picture restorer and publisher, were founder members of the Antique Collectors Club. They live in a Sussex village near Hastings and Rye, seaside towns which, with Brighton, often feature in his novels.